THE
IRON
FAE

THE IRON FAE

THE TWISTED CROWN SERIES

A.K. KOONCE & REBECCA GREY

CONTENTS

ONE

A SEX TOY RUSE

I'm safe.

Safety is the goal right now, but it doesn't feel comforting when I'm walking out on Lincoln, walking away from Jase. I no longer have a safety net to fall on, it's just me.

Lincoln let me go. Lincoln *arranged* it.

My heart sinks further into my twisted stomach, filling it with confusing and messy emotions.

I shouldn't have left.

I should have fought.

I should have—

My long fingers push through my hair in a rush and I try to focus as my attention drifts up to the bright eyes of the Prince of the Iron Court. The castle doors are close enough to touch. Just behind them is an uncertain future and a last resort sort of welcome.

But Kai doesn't reach for the doors. My train wreck appearance is captivating all of his attention.

"Mother despises untidiness," he murmurs as he continues picking through my locks like a mother monkey fussing over its little one.

I've never met his mother, *Lincoln's mother*. I wonder if he looks like her. Will her face be familiar? Will she catch the smell of her son still clinging to my skin from our hungry good-bye?

"Am I going to meet her?" I ask, my voice lost on the passing breeze.

Kai's touch softens. After a heartbeat, he grazes the sides of my cheeks and grips my shoulders. His golden gaze settles on me with pity.

I don't want to be pitied.

"No. Most certainly not, if we can avoid it."

I nod, wringing my hands together in front of me. I don't have the strength to return his gaze or the want to witness how sorry he may or may not feel for me. It's doubtful that queens often receive pity so I might as well get used to it now.

Darkness shrouds the castle, the only light coming from the nearness of the moon and the sparkle of the stars. Bugs hiss in the trees. Animals cooing and calling to one another off in the forest. A howl erupts from the edge of the woods, stark silver eyes watching us from the brush. My body jumps from its mere proximity and the volume of which it calls out.

"I wish I could say it's safer inside," Kai chuckles.

Safe. Lincoln said this would be safe.

Nothing is truly safe when the ruling queen wants you dead.

"Mother can be quite the handful which is why we mustn't tell her what or whom you are yet. I'll keep you away but if anybody asks, I've brought you here from the human world as my guest," Kai continues. His firm grasp drops from my shoulders and he reaches for the doors.

"Am I staying in the Library? In the pocket world?"

"I've arranged for you to have your own guest suite. My very human guest. Rowan should have it ready now." He hovers with his hand touching the door, unworried about the beasts that linger on the edge of the woods that border the castle.

My attention drifts to the fringe of their property. No guards. No high walls. It's all a testament to their powers. They don't need the extra security because no one would dare defy them.

Another howl pierces the air. I look back into the silver gaze that watches us. Between blinks, a few more pairs of eyes appear. Still, I watch back. No part of me feels intimidated any longer. Perhaps it's the deflating apathy and disassociation consuming me that leaves little room for anything else.

"When the tides of the ocean rise to drown out the beaches of your life you have a few choices you can make. Recede and hide from the waters till the tide lowers, drown in the waters, or build a boat and float," Kai whispers.

Lincoln hates his stupid metaphors. My first thought. *I don't mind them.* My second.

"Maybe I should opt for option number four." I straighten my slumped shoulders.

"I didn't give you four options." A blatant and brilliant smile lifts his cheeks.

"I'm making a fourth option."

"And...?"

"And maybe I'll be the sun. Maybe I'll shine so bright, so hot, so persistently that my heat will evaporate what was meant to drown the beaches." It's my own shameful attempt at a metaphor. Stupid, I know. But it feels right in this moment. It feels like something Kai will understand.

His tongue runs over his white teeth and his smile returns more devilish than moments before. "That's my girl." Flat against the iron doors, he presses his palm and the door eases open.

No light greets us in the long empty hallway. Not a single book either. I sigh, flooded with relief. Not the pocket realm. I'm not trapped.

Underneath Kai's icy blonde ponytail I can see the ends of his iron crescent tattoo on the base of his neck peek out. His steps make no sound as he moves but mine are clumsy, annoyingly human, and embarrassingly loud as they echo. Still no guards.

Unlike the pocket realm, these halls are made of black painted stone. Or maybe they are not painted... but charred. The occasional window is tinted purple, casting its glow onto the black and white checkered tiles. Kai turns the corner and the long stretch of hall ends in a curtained balcony. What sort of view would I have if I stood at its ledge?

A shadowed figure slinks out in front of us, all curves and thin pointed features. For two tense seconds I'm worried it's their mother. But the low snickering laugh that hisses from her lips instantly suggests otherwise.

"Violet," Kai says bitterly. "Why? Why must you always hide in the shadows like some sinister feline?"

"The Mortal Queen," She half seethes, half sings. "I knew Rowan was darting around the halls like he had a secret to hide. What are we telling Mother?"

"We weren't going to tell Mother anything."

"You weren't going to tell me anything either but if I could figure out that the two of you idiots are prancing around the castle trying to hide the object of Cordelia's obsession then I'm sure Mother can too."

Kai lifts his chin. His hands tremble at his side and he reaches into his pocket, no doubt stroking the bottle of Reminints.

I step around his side, eyeing the Princess. She eyes me back. Her slender body is fitted with the slip of a sheer grey dress. Her nipples and bikini area are only covered by the tiniest pieces of black fabric underneath. My attention lingers too long. Not on the perfection that is the Princess's form but on the strange idea that this woman's vagina is near nonexistent. If I wore that, one of my lady lips would we waving out the side of those panties. I didn't know coochies that small existed. I suppose in this perfect Fae world they do.

Damn, I want a Fae vagina.

Violet hums and places her hands on her hips. "Human girl. Mortal Queen. What are we doing with you?"

Hide me. Train me. Help me release my powers. Teach me about your family. An endless list comes quickly to mind. My lips part to respond, to let her know that I haven't a clue where to start. But Kai jumps in.

"Cordelia found a seer who can delve into the darkest parts of her mind."

Violet's eyebrows reach for her hairline. "You mean into Lincoln's mind."

"Right."

"She's here to protect Lincoln." She drops her arms, spinning on her heel. "Why didn't you just say that?"

"She's here to protect her too. If Cordelia found out exactly who she was she'd be next up on the public chopping block." Kai starts down the hall again after his sister.

"Don't you think she'll put two and two together now that I'm not around at all?" I interject.

"Obviously. But she wouldn't dare think to come for you here. To suggest that we have you at all would be an utter insult."

"Plus, Mother would never knowingly allow you." Violet's bare feet are but a whisper against the floor. It feels purposeful, as if she's making herself less of what she is so that I would feel less unsteady. Surprising considering how unnerving she can be. "What are we telling her?"

"I found Briar on a trip to the human world. She... intrigues me."

"Ha," Violet coughs. "How does it feel to be passed off to our Mother as Kai's human play thing? Don't let Lincoln know, I doubt he would enjoy the thought."

"Play thing," I say slowly. A puppet on his string?

"Fae don't bring humans here for fun unless it's for sexual favors," she continues, "Don't get caught by Mommy or she might make you prove that's why you are here."

My next breath is caught in my lungs. I practically choke on it.

"Don't say that to her," Kai coos.

"It's true." She stops, pointing a pointed finger toward the door. "I'm assuming this room that Rowan thoroughly had readied is for the girl?"

Both their faces, schooled into cool confidence turn to me. A soft wind blows the curtains from the balcony that is near enough now I could run to it and throw myself over the edge without them even registering it. It feels like my only moment to run. Even if the two of them look at me as if I'm more prey than predator, I have to quell those anxious thoughts.

Through the split in the curtain the moon casts its light across the floor. The glow of it arcs against the tile reaching the bottom of the guest suite's door. Like a sign. Or like what I wish was a sign that entering this room, so far away from Lincoln, is still the right thing to do.

"This is her room." Kai reaches for the doorknob.

"I'll let you two have your alone time," she purrs, stealing away back into the shadows. My blurry human eyes can't pick out her form as soon as she recedes, leaving me with the unnerving feeling of being watched by the unseen.

The door opens softly, Kai's hand pressing to the small of my back to guide me inside. There is a warmth to the room, a coziness that tingles over my skin as I enter. Just what exactly is the Fae magic inside this room meant to do?

With a flick of his iron stained fingers, Kai flips the lights on. The room isn't so much of a guest suite as it is a whole home by itself. A sparkling chandelier dripping in lavender colored pendants hangs centered over a small four chair table that's polished to an immaculate shine. Bookshelves are set inside the walls in two slim pentagons bordered by the same metal as the rest of the high-pitched ceilings. The large window directly in front of us is tinted much the same as the rest, deep royal purple. I can hardly make out the twinkle of the stars on the other side.

I step around the table, running my fingers over the high-backed chairs and brushing the floral velvet material of the cushions. A fireplace burns ever so slightly where the room recesses down a single step. The black pelt of some large unrecognizable animal is laid down on the checkered floor. Surrounding that are two long couches, decorated with round metallic pillows that reflect the warmth of the light. A love seat sits between the couches catching the majority of the fire's out put, another fur pelt strung across its back.

Stepping down into the living space, I look behind it. Three large pointed windows line the back wall. A long, large bed covered in the same pelts and quilts and sparkling metallic or velvet fabrics waits. Two sconces on the walls between the windows glow around it lighting up a pair of side tables.

To the left there are two doors. I stare at them.

"Bathroom and closet," Kai says softly, still standing behind me at the door. The door is closed and his back is pressed against it but I didn't even hear it shut.

"Oh," I whisper, walking up to brush my finger against the bed frame. It's metal that curls into intricate designs at the head and foot of the bed. I half expect the touch to burn or instantly blister but the bed is not iron. Thankfully.

"The closet is empty, but I'll arrange for that to be amended tomorrow."

Biting my lip, I sit on the edge of the mattress. Clipped to either side of the headboard, dangles two sets of... handcuffs. I narrow my gaze on them before turning to Kai. His face remains neutral but the tips of his ears burn.

He clears his throat, pulling out the Reminints and

slipping a petal to his tongue. "This, uh, is typically, um, for my guests."

"You often handcuff them?" I half way smile.

He blinks. "Yes. If they are willing."

"So... I'm your... sex guest?"

"No. But yes," he says all too quickly, "It's just a ruse."

My eyelids feel heavy, stinging in the way that suggests that I've cried, even though no tears have left my eyes. I don't have time to cry over my situation or to ponder what's between me and Lincoln. Not today. Maybe tomorrow. Maybe next week. Who knows how long I'll be a guest of the Iron Court for?

"Why do we have to lie to your mother?"

Kai takes a tentative step forward, then shakes his head as if rethinking and steps back once again. "May I join you?" he finally asks.

"Yeah."

"Yeah." He mimics my plain accent, taking away from his beautifully smooth one. "That sounds so... churlish."

"You forget I wasn't raised as royalty." I run my fingers through the fur underneath me.

Quietly, with the tails of his fine suit jacket trailing behind him, he walks through the living space and up to the bed. He stops with many feet still between us, examining me before he looks over the room.

"Our *Mother* does not take kindly to Shadow Fae. She has little love for Lincoln, or patience for that matter.

As a human, full blooded and ignorant, you're welcome for play. It's quite common amongst royalty to take in human subs. Why else do you think so many Shadow Fae exist?"

I swallow. So that's the kind of partner Kai is. Though, I try not to think too hard on it, I glance back at the handcuffs then down to the foot of the bed where I find two more.

"My father, though, he is of lesser power than Mother, the weight of the court's decisions do not fall on him. He has found love in his heart for Lincoln, a child that is not even his."

"He seemed nice enough." I think back to our brief encounter in the pocket realm.

"Yes, I suppose." Kai's eyes fall to near slits, his shoulders relaxing as he breathes out the effects of the Reminints.

"Will Violet say anything?"

He looks back up to me, his face riddled with confusion as if he forgot I was even in the room at all. "No. No, most certainly not. However, it would be naïve of us to assume that she won't use the ruse to her advantage or for her entertainment." Kai sways on his feet for a moment before he perks up. "I'll leave you for some rest. Do you need anything before I go? I could call for whatever you'd like. As my guest my offerings to you will not be hindered and you'll find yourself without want or need any longer."

"I...no. I'm okay."

He stares. "You don't feel safe?"

My fingers curl into my palm. It's not that I don't feel safe it's just that this entire new realm is the *unknown*.

"I'll be okay. I'm just nervous."

His shining shoes drag forward, his head tilted as he examines my facial expression. With now steady hands he reaches behind him pulling something from the back of his pants. As he brings it to the light, I realize it's a small dagger. He tosses the blade in the air, perfectly balancing the point in his fingertips as he offers me the hilt. Purple stones and black stones alike shine along the handle.

"For you, to ease some of your worry." He lets me delicately take it from him. I balance it in my palms. Kai turns toward the door walking a few steps before he pauses and looks back at me.

I pull my gaze from the weapon, cold and hard in my grasp.

"Please, don't use it on me." His face goes blank. "I'm trusting you as you must trust me."

TWO

RAG DOLL

THE HILT of the blade still rests in my palm. Every stone buried in the magnificent weapon's metal is also pressed into my skin, leaving behind their marks. Still, I can't bring myself to release my tight hold. It's my only defense.

Sleep hasn't come much in the night. The large bed, with its many blankets and covers still feels cold. Every noise is a new danger that makes my eyes flutter open only to stare at the door that never opens. It's not particularly safe to sleep with a sharp dagger in the bed, but it feels safer than having to take the time to reach for it.

My eyes feel groggy, sleep begging my body to give in, but my mind keeps racing. I don't want to think. I want just a moment to be numb and lost to the feelings that make my chest tight and my heart ache that much more. Maybe that's too much to ask.

Sunlight filters through the purple windows casting

the royal color across the room. The fire has long since turned to embers.

I roll to my stomach. Stretching, I point the knife at the still dangling handcuffs. With a flick of my wrist, the blade slips into the cuff. I let it drop with a quiet *clank* against the black rails. It's a bewildering thought. Never in my years, or in the short time that I'd known Kai, would I suspect him to be that type of man. Now that I know it, I can totally see it. It's always the quiet ones.

A brief knock sounds at the door. With a sharp inhale, I push myself up and turn to face the door, still under the covers. The dagger presses against the bed, the point of the blade poking a hole into the sheets underneath me. *Damn it.*

"Yes?" I call. My answer is pointless though as the door swings open at the exact moment Rowan breezes in followed by Kai.

"I told him not to barge in," Kai sighs.

"I told my brother that you and I are on a first name basis and the pleasantries are unnecessary." Rowan drops himself onto the sofa. He looks at the ashy fireplace with a frown. Snapping his fingers, a full flame fire roars inside the hearth casting its glow across the floor and onto his smudged boots.

"Good morning to you too." I say, placing the dagger in my lap.

"See? She is still a lady." Kai fiddles with the buttons of his silver suit. "Good morning, Briar." He breathes, clearly exasperated by his brother, and gestures toward the still open door. "Breakfast?"

A thin boned servant girl, with thin straight hair hanging around her round face, tiptoes into the room holding a bed tray. Steam rolls off the food, fanning behind her like her own personal storm cloud. She takes careful steps down into the living space and then back up toward the bed. Kai follows her, frowning at Rowan as he passes.

As they reach the bedside the girl looks down at the knife in my lap then up to my face. She repeats the questioning look until Kai steps beside her with a tense smile.

"You won't be needing that for breakfast." He plucks the weapon from my hand and sets it against the bedside table, allowing the servant to set the bed tray across my lap before she darts away. "We have actual silverware for you to use that would be easier than cutting your eggs with a family heirloom."

"It seems you have more than one brother eating out of the palm of your hand, Briar." Rowan sings, picking at his nails.

I take a deep breath. The sweetest scents of the warm syrup covered pancakes assault my senses, accompanied by the perfectly savory and crispy bacon. There are no mortal girls to poison here. I shouldn't worry about being poisoned, right?

Kai finally releases a long-held breath as I pick up a piece of bacon and begin absently chewing. My mind still twists and turns around the prospect of who, why, and how the mortal girls were being poisoned. Kai pulls his small vial of petals from his coat, offering one to me. I shake my head. He smiles softly, shaking a few leaves to his tongue before putting the container back into his pocket.

He is never short of his supply. I remember the fleeting moment, so smooth I hardly caught it, when Bellion slipped the prince his addiction. ...*the best herbologist in the realm*... Could Bellion and his blind loyalty be behind it all? No one is more loyal, more catering to the queen's whim than the tall billowy man.

My chewing slows as I process my own revelation. If that's true, this food is safe. I pick up the fork and cut a chunk of pancake, shoving it into my mouth.

"You look angry." Rowan sits forward.

"What?"

"You've got your eyes all narrowed." Kai pitches in, propping himself on the edge of the bed frame.

I'm thankful neither of these men have a view into my mind or the front row seat to any of my thoughts. Instantly, my mind reaches for the tether between me and Lincoln. He's there, quiet and reserved, his mental fingers no longer reaching into my thoughts so actively.

"Sorry, I'm just lost in thought."

A drop of syrup drips from the fork, stuffed with yet another bite, and falls to my shirt. I'd slept in the clothes I had arrived in. My necklace, my power as Lincoln called it, still warm in my pocket.

"As my guest, everyone will expect for you to be...

appropriately dressed. Humans typically are thrilled to wear gowns and otherwise much more proper attire..."

"I'm not your typical human."

"No, you are not." Rowan says.

Kai glances over his shoulder looking down at his brother who only stares back at me. "Be that as it may, I've arranged for Violet to take you down to our finest dress shops to pick up an assortment of gowns and whatever else you'd wish."

Any smile I may have held falters at the idea of spending time with Violet.

"Don't worry, I'll tag along so that witchling sister of ours doesn't eat you alive." Rowan adds.

"How reassuring." I look to Kai. "And you?"

"I will be here. Working for the morning."

I bob my head. Kai pulls himself up from the bed heading for the door. Before he passes his brother, he stoops to whisper something in his ear. Rowan agrees with a halfhearted, "uh-huh" and a roll of his pretty golden eyes.

"I'll fetch Violet." Kai purses his lips at the door. "Please, do try to enjoy yourself today, Briar."

Nothing in the Fae world is rushed or worried or overthought. In my mortal mind it is, though. How do I enjoy myself when I know the shadow queen is after me? She's surely noticed my absence by now. My cousin is still in her court without a home. And the Fae I've relied on to protect me, the one I've developed these strangling, unwanted feelings for, is so far away. His mind feeling even more distant than that.

When the silence between us lingers, Kai finally steps out of the room. He pulls the door closed behind him. My eyes fall to my food that I eat to my fill. Rowan watching me without a word as I do.

My hands wrap around the handles of the tray to lift it from my lap so I may stand. Rowan waves a hand, the entire thing disappearing.

"Let me help with that." He grins.

"Thanks."

His gaze eats me up. Every inch of my skin is already sick of him watching me, though I know it could be worse. Why am I even boohooing about a handsome Fae man finding me attractive enough to dote on? Attractive enough to want to marry?

"Are you still decidedly set on wooing me?" I say with a calculated languidness. I think back on the blur of the night in the Lavender Lounge of the brief kiss we shared. While the Fae technically spark, us humans look for chemistry. Rowan and I... we have it... but not in the truly shocking, electrical way that Lincoln and I do. Rowan's kisses don't satisfy the longing need inside of me.

"I'm here aren't I?" He shrugs. "I could be off fucking anyone else but instead I'm chasing after you. Seems like I might not be the only one either. But I don't mind the competition. It's healthy."

"And do you see me as a prize?"

"Absolutely."

Yeah, I fucking hate that.

I don't take the time to respond as I press my feet into my boots. Before I move toward him, I take the time to slip the amulet into a small pot on top of the fireplace mantel. I pat it for good measure and a wish of safe keeping. There isn't a need for me to reply to Rowan, now, as Violet sweeps into the room without bothering to knock as Rowan had.

"Don't worry, my underdressed pet, I'm here to save you." An emerald green dress wraps around her, tied with a shining satin ribbon. Her tiny feet are slipped into sparkling gold shoes. The heels don't even click against the ground as she moves through the room. It's like she swallows up sound and light.

"If we must." Purposefully, I keep what distance I can between me and Lincoln's sister. I wonder if she is a mirror of her mother's cruel demeanor I'm often told about.

Her eyes narrow on the drop of syrup staining my t-shirt but she doesn't say anything as she glides across the room and takes my hand. In one swift movement she pulls me forward from the bed and drags me as I clumsily follow. Rowan snickers behind us. Even with his echoed laugh I can sense him trail after us.

Outside of the room the halls are illuminated by the light of the day. I watch door after door pass only to wonder which one they'll drag me through to portal me all the way to whatever shop meets their fancy.

I feel like a rag doll. Their plaything. Even if it's all for my safety, I despise the way I feel like I'm just floating along. *But what sort of coming into myself sort of story would it be if they didn't whisk me away for some sort of makeover?* I think bitterly.

Violet's grip holds me with a surprising delicateness. She holds onto me until her unheard heels pause at the chosen door. We stop and I look around. This hall looks the same as the last and the one before it. I could get lost here so easily, and it's only now that I realize that I don't know how exactly we got here.

Twisting, I look back at Rowan as his sister reaches for the door. His attention is fixed much lower than I'd care for it to be. He meets my gaze with a knowing smirk and steps forward as Violet tugs me into the void. In the briefest of moments, I reach out to him. Not because I feel any need for his touch, or because I'm nervous it will be just Violet and I, though I am. Simply, it's because I haven't figured out how to land and with what I know of the Princess she isn't likely to catch me or to care.

We fall. The three of us descend into the abyss of the portal, sinking like abandoned ships. Violet's palm pulls away from mine and even in the darkness I can tell she's grinning. Even as I lose the gentle touch she'd given me, I reach out hopeful.

Fingers graze up my forearm, holding me steady. As my head spins, I know the landing is coming. I dread embarrassing myself in front of Violet. Rowan won't let that happen. The air between us is choked away and he brings me up to his body. Even through the many layers of clothes his muscles are apparent.

It's enough, the moment long enough, I can close my eyes and pretend it's Lincoln. As soon as his messy curls and deep-set dimples appear inside my head, Rowan stumbles forward, holding me. And Lincoln's gone.

I crack my eyes open. Rowan tilts his head, letting me go slowly. Violet's already strolling down a pathed walkway with racks of elaborate clothes set out that she's examining with such scrutiny.

"I may not be able to read minds," Rowan tracks after Violet. "but I can smell the difference in you when you think about Lincoln."

"You can smell that?" Suddenly, I'm resisting the urge to lift my arm and take a whiff of my own armpit.

"Humans put off a lot of pheromones. You don't consciously recognize it but we can."

"Well, I really don't like that."

I frown at the scarf Violet holds looking between the material and myself. She plucks it off the hanger and drapes it over her torso so it covers her chest. Not a scarf, just a barely there top.

"It'd look better on me anyway." She shrugs.

"What's so great about Lincoln?" Rowan tries again.

"I don't know. He's kind, funny—though I'm not going to tell him. He's loyal and loving. Protective but not suffocating." *He has a good dick.* I think to myself. "Lincoln believes in me more than I believe in me."

"I believe in you."

21

"You believe in my status." I snort.

"I believe in that ass too." Rowan wiggles his brows.

"Exactly." Violet rolls her eyes. "It's comments like those that put women off."

"They seem to work well enough when I'm taking them to bed." Rowan points to a shop with its dangling sign. The dressmaker.

"Let's make this very clear." Violet strolls ahead pushing open the door to the shop. A bell rings inside. "Any woman, when she sleeps with you, made that decision long before you did."

"What do you mean?"

"I mean, if you think women are always silky smooth and smell like cherry blossoms, then you're an idiot."

I catch a laugh in the palm of my hand as Violet responds. Rowan shrugs with indifference. He holds the door for me and waves me inside. The shop quickly reminds me of Cordelia's dressmaker and our visit there, except more organized. Dresses are arranged by color across racks that line walls on either side. Within one color they are organized by sheer coverage, the first dresses being thongs that basically are held up by your shoulders instead of your hips, in my opinion.

An attendant sits behind a desk, he bows as we walk in. Other than the ring of the bell there is no ushering welcome or designer waiting to pin fabric to me while I stand uncomfortably as if I've never worn a dress before. It's hardly meeting my minimum expectations for a movie like makeover.

"So what kind of dresses do you like?" Violet says. Her hands run down her curves as she watches herself in a large mirror. She hasn't even turned to look at the dresses yet.

"I like as much coverage as I can get." I take my time walking around her looking, but not touching the gowns along the wall.

"Boring!" Rowan huffs.

"Rowan is right, *for once*. Why don't you want to show a little bit of skin?" She pauses her peruse through her own reflection long enough to look me head to toe. "You're pretty enough."

Pretty enough. I imagine that's as close to a compliment as I'm going to get with Violet. And I'll take it.

"I don't know. I'm just not comfortable with it. Humans don't typically walk around in lingerie ball gowns."

The walls seem a little bit closer than they had just moments ago. The dresses multiplying every time I look.

"Human's don't blah blah blah. You're in the Fae realms now, Briar." Rowan pulls a navy blue gown with a plunge that reaches for the navel and two strips of fabric that are supposed to act as the skirt and somehow cover up my lady bits. "We're buying this.

I wince as he walks by me to drape the gown over the counter.

"You don't even know my size." I point out.

Violet laughs. "Honey, we don't need your size."

Right. Magic.

23

"What about, like, a pant suit?"

Both the Fae that brought me here and the attendant frown at me. Is that human term? Have I offended them?

"You want to wear a suit like a man?" Violet asks slowly.

"No. Not exactly. There are feminine pant suits..." But even as I say it, I'm aware it's all a lost cause. Their brows are already wrinkled with confusion and outright surprise.

"Let's try this on." Violet devilishly grins.

I'm shaking my head no at the strips of fabric that I can't imagine won't get tangled when I try to slip them onto my body and the sheer fabric that hangs over them when she snaps her fingers. My body jars. The clothing I'd worn here pulls from my body turning to dust in the air. Underneath it the dress is already fitted to my curves. One thick strap runs over my nipples, many smaller ones spider webbing to make up the remainder of the bra. I clutch my thighs together. A small piece of material runs between my legs. I'm about to have a lip slip. Bands wrap around my hips holding it all in place underneath a sheer dark plum coverup that hugs my chest and peplums at my waist, with a skirt that stops mid-thigh.

A squeak admits from my gaping mouth. My arms wrap around me, trying to hold my body in. Violet gives me an unapologetic smirk.

"No, no, no." She clicks her tongue. "Move your hands." Her thin fingers pry my grip from my body as she steers me toward the mirror. "You should work on your confidence. You look so much better now. In fact, you're wearing this home."

"That's hardly necessary." I wheeze. "I am confident."

"Then you won't mind wearing this out." Violet stiffens, turning back to look through the racks.

I chance a glance at Rowan. His arms hold a heap of outfits, each one as revealing as the next. Moisture shines on his lips, following the slip of his tongue. He stares so concentratedly at me that it feels as if he is seeing into my soul, or trying to.

You look… edible. Lincoln's deep husky voice enters my mind in an abrupt startling way.

I jump, turning back to the mirror. Gently, I run my hands over the thin fabric.

Can you see me?

I can see you, how you see you, through your eyes.

I can tell Lincoln's distracted, hardly available for our conversation, barely connected to the moment. My palms get sweaty with a new, odd sort of nervousness.

I haven't heard from you today. It's the less clingy dramatic version of 'I miss you.' Hours feel like days, almost weeks, when I'm so used to his commentary inside my head. With a deep breath, I try to take myself in as everyone else sees me. I've never thought myself ugly. You'd think with the number of people telling me that I'm endlessly beautiful I'd have a big head. It's just I'm so… naked.

Busy. Just stopping in to suggest that you tell Rowan to shut his mouth and find something else to look at.

A humming laugh vibrates my chest. I move stiffly, worried the bands of material will slip in either an unflattering way or full out expose me.

"Rowan," I clear my throat, giving him some time to bring his attention up to my face. "Lincoln seems to think that you should close your mouth and find yourself occupied with something other than my ass."

Couldn't have said it better myself.

"Isn't he busy running errands for Cordelia?" Rowan purses his lips but turns on the heel of his boot.

"Ouch." I mumble wondering if Lincoln can hear what I hear too. Maybe it's just an echo of my thoughts as I process it.

You jealous? I ask.

Hmm, no. Just hate to see Rowan drooling over you. How embarrassing for him.

Of course. I smile to myself. An image flashes through my head. It's me but not as I see me with all my flaws. Instead it's how Lincoln sees me.

And I'm beautiful. Truly, endlessly so.

My breaths become shallow as another image flashes through my mind. This one is blurry. A scenario made from one's imagination.

Lincoln stands behind me, running a hand down my arm. He turns me to face him. It flashes and I'm lowered to my knees, my lips locked around his cock.

My eyes widen and my cheeks burn painfully red.

Lincoln Ziko.

What? He asks so innocently I'm unsure even he is aware of what he's shared. Then his rumbling laughter follows. *Don't let your panties get too wet, Rowan will sniff that out faster than Violet got you into that apparatus in the first place.*

I try not to think too hard on the way I'm overly aware of my body and the wind that touches far too much of my skin. I try to be as confident as I need to be to pull off this attire that they consider so normal.

The attendant admires all of their choices as they magically fold into their bags. Violet hands them off to Rowan who looks pleased by the options. *At least he likes them. That makes one of us.*

"Let's hurry home. I'm sure Kai wants to see the bill he is footing and the outfits we picked out for his little play thing." The Princess sings cheerfully.

I swallow, trying to ease the dryness of my throat and follow them from the shop. I can only hope that Kai doesn't treat me like his *play thing.* I'm not sure my acting skills are good enough for that.

At the mention of Kai's name Lincoln's presence in my mind goes quiet, hidden behind his thick and sturdy wall. My small smile fades as he does.

THREE

NEARLY NAKED AND VERY AFRAID

Every step I take my thighs rub forcibly together. There is no humanly way my walk can be attractive when I'm scared to un-pinch the fabric I'm gripping together my lady canal. I'm not sure the universe was ready for me and my 'endless beauty', just as I'm not ready for it. I sure as hell am not beautiful now.

My head still feels dizzy from our abrupt arrival back at the castle. Still, Violet and Rowan wheel me ahead. This time I try to take in the hallways, to memorize some sort of path or escape route if necessary, but I wasn't imagining it when I realized the hallways all look exactly the same. No matter which way you turn there are an assortment of doors broken up only by a few lavender tinted windows and at the end of the hall a large balcony. Though, in the day the wispy curtains are drawn back allowing the sun and the mild weather into the castle.

"Kai is going to flip when he sees you." Violet grins.

She pulls me to a stop just short of what I'm assuming is Kai's office and makes a show of fiddling with my hair. I try not to stare into her iron tainted gaze but she's as much mesmerizing as she is wicked and undoubtedly deadly.

"Don't stare too long," she whispers, "wouldn't want you falling in love with me."

My eyes flair, my cheeks turning a brilliant shade of red. I'm not so much as attracted to Violet as I am intrigued by the way she holds herself. Jealous. I'm minimally jealous.

"Lincoln would never allow that," Rowan says bitterly, already leaning into the door.

"You all forget that Lincoln isn't my boss and I'll damn well fall in love with whomever I wish." I tug the sheer fabric down as if that will hide all the skin poking out from the strips of fabric underneath.

"Okay." The Prince scoffs before calling to his brother. "Kai, we've brought you a sexy little toy."

"I'll pretend as if it's necessary for you to call her that when no one else is around. But I'm sure our Mortal Queen would enjoy just an ounce more of respect." Kai pinches his nose between his index finger and his thumb.

My boots have long since been replaced with what I would consider stripper heels. They're far too tall, and the heel far too skinny for my incoordination. I shuffle forward.

Kai blinks, letting go of his nose. He looks from me to his siblings then back to me, swallowing hard.

"Playing the part well? Right, brother?" Rowan purrs, melting against the door as it closes behind him.

Kai adverts his gaze back down to his desk. "You look stunning. Absolutely playing into the ruse."

"Do you not like it?" It's almost a hopeful question. If it doesn't please him then maybe I could slip into something that's actually more comfortable.

His eyes pan from my feet slowly up to my face. The right side of his mouth edges up into a smirk. "It's perfect."

Double damn it.

"Now that we have your keeper's approval, perhaps I can give her a tour?" Rowan suggests.

"What are you doing?" I say quickly, stepping closer to Kai's desk.

His hand rests with a pen pressed to a long document that he scribbles over. A few books are stacked together, one propped open against the pile with a feather stuffed between the pages. Kai drops the pen and runs his hand over his outfit. It's less flashy than usual, a dull brown jacket over a cream-colored billowing blouse.

"I'm about to leave for a little hunt with a few Dukes bidding for my attention."

"I love to hunt," I rush to say. Then I try not to scrunch up my face with the rotten feeling of the lie afterwards.

Kai leans back in his chair, both hands flat against the desk. Violet looks appalled at the very idea and Rowan arches a skeptical brow.

"It would look good for our ruse for me to come along, yes?"

"I mean, yes. If it pleases you so, who am I to decline the offer of being in your presence?" Kai stands, accessing my outfit in a new scrutinous way. "You'll have to sit side saddle."

I'm not even sure I know how to get up on a horse by myself. But sure, I can hang off the side of one and not fall off. How hard can it be?

"I can do that."

"You'd rather go for a hunt than tour the castle?" Rowan drawls.

"I'll be here plenty long enough for you to give me the grand tour. Right? We can go tomorrow." *No offense, Rowan, but I'm desperate for an escape. Every second spent with you and Violet feels like a dangerous opportunity for one of you to pick the meat off my bones.*

"Tour tomorrow, then," Kai confirms. He brushes back a loose strand of blonde hair from his face and smiles weakly. "So scurry along now, you two surely have something better you could be doing right now." He waves off his siblings.

Violet may have something better to do, and she seems unaffected by the dismissal as she slides out the door. Rowan, on the other hand, he seems to have nothing but time available to him. Rowan's face falls to a neutral expression. He stuffs his hands into the pocket of his long jacket and walks out the door.

I let loose a sigh.

"So did you hunt much in the human realm?" Kai looks down as he speaks. He reaches under his desk, pulling a brown leather belt around his waist. The hilt of a long sword pats against his hip, the blade within the sheath bouncing against his thigh.

"Yeah, all the time."

"Yeah." He mimics my accent like the night before. From under his long lashes he shoots me an impish grin.

"I mean, yes."

Veins in his neck pop out a little as he shrugs out of his jacket. He tugs open a drawer, revealing a baldric he buckles across his chest, another smaller blade protruding from it.

"We use guns." I clear my throat. I'm familiar with guns. I've taken a couple different courses and learned the particular one I keep well enough to take it apart and put it back together. Still, the basics of owning a firearm.

"Guns?" he hums. "That seems... easy."

"You use your blades?" I point.

Kai picks up his jacket and pulls it back over his arms. His honey filled gaze is amused to say the least.

"And magic."

He hovers near me, placing a hand behind my back, but not touching my skin. I'm relieved with the level of respect he offers me. Chewing my lips, I walk beside him. It's a short walk from his office out to the stables.

The warm sun covers my skin in a soothing way as it moves out from behind a cloud. Dark fluffy clouds dot the sky off toward the horizon. We weave through a garden not so much unlike Cordelia's.

A horse is already saddled and ready, tied to a wooden post. Behind the stable is a vast valley, far away from the woods I'd ventured through when I first arrived here. That must have been the back entrance. A few men ride together in the valley, dressed in much similar fashions to Kai atop their horses.

This is when I know I'm way over my head. Though, I probably should have figured that out sooner.

My steps falter, my heels dig into the earth with every step. Sighing, I raise a hand. "I just can't with these. I'm sorry if it makes me less of a lady or look less like I'm here to be your...you know, but I can't." I fuss with the buckles, knowing full and well that I'm probably giving Kai a good show of my fun buns between my legs.

His gaze though is turned toward the men, he's averted his attention, but grips my arm to steady me as I bend. A satisfied moan slips out as I set my bare feet down in the prickly grass.

"Better?" His accent is sweet.

"Much." I hang the shoes from my fingers, not sure what else to do with them. Kai snaps his fingers and they disappear.

"They'll be waiting inside your closet."

I crinkle my nose as we approach and the decaying scent of horse dung greets us. If my human nose is this offended how are the Fae not gagging on it?

"Would you like to ride with me or would you like

your own horse?" He asks, stopping to run his palm down the side of the horse. His stallion is grey with black speckles dotting its fur. The horse's black mane has been cut relatively short, groomed so it's perfectly straight and ends bluntly.

"I don't mind riding with you."

"You don't know anything about horses, do you?" He pats the stallion then closes the distance between us.

"Not at all."

"And hunting?"

"Only a vague idea of the concept." I purse my lips.

He chuckles lightly. "Are my brother and sister so overwhelming that you'd really rather be doing this?"

"No, but yeah. *Yes,* kind of." I wring my hands.

"Duly noted." Kai nods and reaches toward my waist. "May I?"

"Yes."

He grips my sides and lifts me up to the saddle. His hands slip down my legs as I adjust and balance on the horse's back. His smile becomes tense, his gaze following his hands.

You have amazing legs. I remember Lincoln saying. Maybe Lincoln's not the only one to notice.

"It may be better for you, since you're new to this, to straddle. Hopefully it's not too uncomfortable in that outfit."

My hands quiver as I cling to the saddle and pull one leg over it. Nerves burst in popping bubbles inside my stomach. I try my best to ignore them.

Kai sniffles once before he unties the horse from its post and reaches for the horn of the saddle, swinging himself carefully around me. He pushes me forward gently, his legs cupping me and his chest hot against my back. Only the cool metal of his blade within the baldric soothes the heat.

"Ready?" he whispers over my shoulder.

"Never."

He tilts his head with vigorous laughter, pulling the reins and digging his heels into the animal. We lurch forward. Every muscle tightens and I grip the horn tightly, my thighs clench down. Every step the horse makes, I can feel the meat of my body bounce. I'll be lucky if there isn't some sort of nip slip on this trip.

"If you can't relax, I can slip you some Reminints."

"I am relaxed." I squeeze my eyes shut, trying to focus on releasing the tension with little success.

"Are you?" He leans to the side for a better look at my face.

"Yeah!" I say it with too much force and Kai has the nerve to look smug.

"*Yeah.* Yeah. *Yeah.*" He tastes the word over and over again. "I both love it and hate it when you say that."

I'm too scared to respond. The horse's muscles roll underneath us and every movement threatens to pitch me off the side, I swear. Kai's arms cage me in. He's relaxed enough for the both of us.

I focus on my breathing, still trying not to look like I'm nervous. The horse gently trots off toward the valley where the others who wait for us to join finally coming into view.

"Prince Kai, nice of you to finally join us." A man with black braids smiles with brilliant white teeth. He sits on top of a chestnut brown horse who exhales loudly, looking more beastly than tamed.

"What do you have here?" The other man, with his head completely shaved sports a black tattoo made of crescents, much like the one on the back of Kai's neck, circling his scalp. Muscles bulge beneath his form fitted top. He slows his cream-colored stallion as he approaches, looking at me with a suggestive smile.

The Fae breathe in my scent together.

"Human?" The first snickers.

"Her name is Briar. Isn't she lovely?" Kai says plainly.

Both men bob their heads.

"Briar, the goon on the brown horse is Michael. The white one somehow manages to hold up Nicholai. Both are Dukes"

"Lovely to meet you." I smile.

"Oh, and she has manners." Michael raises his brows. "I thought humans were dang near barbaric."

"They have to be, to get in bed with Kai," Nicholai chortles. "She is very pretty. Maybe I'll take her for a spin when you're done."

I can't help but lean back into Kai as Nicholai speaks. I may be here under the pretense that I'm Kai's *special* guest but I am by no means going to be whored out to any other Fae men.

Kai drops a hand to rest on my thigh, his grip lowers toward my knee and he squeezes gently. A show of affection but also a bit of reassurance for me.

"You know I don't share," Kai coos.

"Well with a girl like that." Nicholai bits his lip. "I'll give you time to reconsider when you're done with her."

"It's unlikely that I'll change my mind but you can keep trying to persuade me. I'm partial to bribery." He laughs.

The others laugh with him while I watch with little interest. Kai clicks his tongue and their laughter ceases.

"Very well. What are we on the hunt for today lads?"

"White panther. Seen the beast roaming the wood on multiple occasions as of lately. He has a den nearly dead center. I suggest we split and meet in the middle. If we come across him before we hit the den, call out." Michael steers his horse forward.

A panther. We're hunting a fucking panther. Well he conveniently left that out. I thought I was out for a stroll in the woods while we spy for deer and squirrels. What sort of situation did I just get myself into? Maybe Violet and Rowan were the less deadly option.

"Lovely. Meet you there." Kai smirks at the men, letting out a *whoop* as he yanks the reins and kicks at the horse. We surge past the men and my hair blows behind me.

It's oddly freeing on top of this animal, even if every bump vibrates through me in not always the most pleasant of ways. Kai only slows the gallop as we ease into the woods.

Trees chase up toward the sky, ivy and green vines clinging to their trunks. Soft white flowers bloom at their bases every``` so often, emitting a soft cottony scent. The canopy above nearly blacks out the sun, shading us so much a shiver chases over my skin.

"Are you cold?" His voice is soft. I'd expect him not to want to talk much for fear of warning the panther of our hunt.

"I'm prancing around in just my bra and underwear, practically. What do you think?"

"I'm just being polite." If he is annoyed by my banter he hides it well. He loops the reins over the horn and leans away from me. With a fluid grace he pulls the brown jacket off of him and offers it to me.

"Thank you."

I try to lean forward, create as much space as I can between us to push my arms into the sleeves, but I can only move so far. The soft material of his jacket instantly warms my body. I push my arm roughly through the other sleeve, my knuckles connecting with a loud crack against Kai's face.

"Oof." He grabs his nose.

"Oh my God. Oh my God. I am so sorry." I gasp as I tug the jacket tighter to me. I try to twist to see if I've done any damage, but of course I haven't.

"You really pack a punch, Killer." Kai laughs.

"Seriously, it was an accident."

"Honestly, I probably deserved it. I could use my ego taken down a stroke or two now and again."

"Are you okay?" I whine in a meek voice.

"If your tiny human knuckles could break me then I wouldn't be out riding alone." He picks the reigns back up.

I grip the horn with a pout. Our bodies rock together, carried through the tangle of the forest floor by the horse. I reach forward and delicately touch a strand of its mane. The horse twitches as I brush over it.

In our silence my mind wanders. Yet, my eyes still roam the green for any signs of white fur jumping out to greet us.

How many days will I have to stay in the Iron Court? At what lengths will Cordelia go to find me? They're maddening thoughts. A much scarier reality.

"I, uh, heard that Jase is doing well." Kai softly breaks the anxious worries that pull my brows together.

"Is he?" I sit up straighter. "Have they moved him out of the castle?"

"Yes. I think Lylix has introduced him to a bar owner who had a room available above their business."

Hopefully, he doesn't drink his days away...

"Do...uh, do you and Jase talk often?" We keep our voices low.

"I mean, yes. Jase's letters are often very long and wordy. He sure does love to talk." Kai blinks. "I find him very... interesting."

"I'm sure Jase would be down to be your human

guest." My lips curl at the thought. It's gross that I've even suggested it, honestly.

Birds caw overhead, taking flight from a branch high above us. Wind rustles the brush where smaller animals hide. The forest has a heartbeat all its own.

"Jase is Shadow Fae, so it's a little bit different."

"Right."

"He is much like you, though. Very attractive."

"I'm sure he just eats that right up when you say it. If you're kind to him, you'll always have a friend. Jase is very loyal, you know?"

"I know." A shadow of a smile graces his lips.

The Shadow Court seems to hold multiple things that feel an awful lot like home to me. I feel hollow so far away from them both. It's only a matter of time though, I console myself.

As much as I'd noticed the sounds of the wildlife, soothing in their own way, I quickly notice when all sounds come to a sudden halt. Even the horse's breaths below us are shallow and quiet. The breeze stops. All of nature is suddenly aware of something I'm not.

I look from side to side, nothing but green, dense trees. Kai pulls a hand back to his baldric.

"Be very still." He advises.

I don't move. I can't. Not with the steady beating of adrenaline pulsing through me. My ears strain to hear anything. Only silence follows.

A blur of white flashes across our path. There, and gone in an instant. Kai grunts softly, sending his blade flying in practiced rotations through the air. It hits as the animal stops in front of us.

An outlandish hiss responds to the puncture of the blade sticking out from the panther's ribs. But this animal... the *panther*... stands at eye level with us while we are seated on top of our horse. It hunches forward, baring its sharp teeth at us. Its hide is thick with clumps of fur protruding here and there along its arching back.

Then it charges.

DAMP PANTIES

Kᴀɪ ʏᴀɴᴋs ᴀᴛ ᴛʜᴇ ʀᴇɪɴs, the horse following smoothly. Teeth gnash in the space we once occupied. An unyielding, terror-filled scream slowly dies on my lips as we ride away. The forest crashes behind us, with the beast clambering over anything in its way.

"Alright, Cupcake, if the boys didn't know where we were before they sure do now," Kai says with a grunt as he leans forward with the horse. "Here, hold this."

His steady hands drop the reins in my sweaty palms, still trembling from the sudden shock. I hold the leather, a desperate refusal ready to leave my lips but Kai dives off the side of the horse.

No. Not dives... off.

I'm screaming again fearful he's just left me to gallop off alone into the woods to face an elephant size feline but he merely swings himself around and sits with his back to me in the saddle.

That's some fancy fucking foot work when we are moments away from being split open by footlong claws.

The blade of his sword shines from a sliver of light that's managed to break the canopy above. It sings as the sharpened blade cuts through the air, slashing at the cat.

Kai tilts his head back in a wicked laugh.

"How can you be laughing at a time like this?"

"We're fine!" He pushes me to the side with him, dodging a swiping white paw.

"Are we?!" It's a squeaky shriek. "I think I may have just pissed my pants."

"We can wring out your damp panties when we're done."

My ears are flooded with the cracking of twigs, limbs, and fallen debris underneath the beating hooves of our horse. Hisses and fearsome roars are met with Kai's throaty grunts and the whistle of his sword. Somewhere off behind us another chorus emerges. A thankful sound. Two horses galloping in near unison appear behind the panther.

Cheers rally from Michael's and Nicholai's throats. Both of them reach for their weapons. Arrows cut through the air, flying at a speed so quick, my human eyes only see the pull of the string and the arrow head buried within the feline's thick pelt. Michael flashes his glowing smile as the panther stops its chase after us and turns back to the two Fae behind it.

"Slow the horse," Kai says over his shoulder.

"As if I know how to do that." I grit my teeth.

"Pull the reins toward you. Then turn us around. You know what, let me just..." He pushes his sword back into his belt, reversing the trick he performed earlier and swinging himself back up into the seat to face me. Sweat has pooled on his neck and chest making my shoulders damp as he reaches around me. "Here."

Trotting back to the men takes only a moment. The panther's blood dots its pelt making it a stark cherry red near the wounds and the rest of its fur a mulled strawberry milk color. Breakfast turns over in my stomach. I can't watch. I don't want to watch.

"Thought you might have taken off there for a second, Prince Kai. It's practically licking its wounds now," Nicholai calls.

Large round shoulder blades poke out of the animals back as it lowers to the ground watching the pair. Michael points a notched arrow at the cat, watching with narrowed eyes.

"You're shaking," Kai says with surprise, his eyebrows pinching together.

"I think I'm going to puke." I manage, still clinging to the saddle.

I expect an annoyed sigh or even the complaint that I've ruined the hunt all together. It's what my ex-boyfriend Collin would have done. Collin probably would have even considered pushing me from the horse and letting me find my way back to the castle through the dense forest just so he could have some fun.

"Close your eyes," Kai says firmly.

"Wh—"

"Just do it. I'll tell you when you can open again."

I take a deep breath, to calm the urge to yak inside my lap, then close my eyes. Kai shifts, the snap of his fingers followed by an even louder crack. Adrenaline still pulses inside my veins, making each inhale shaky. There is a final cheer from the other Fae.

The horse turns, pointing us in the opposite direction. We ride in silence for a few paces before Kai softly says, "You can open your eyes now."

We sway together with every revolution of the horse's steps. There is an unfamiliar tang to the air. I don't dwell on the thought.

"Thank you." Is all I can offer.

"Don't worry about it. Mind if we take the scenic route so you have time to calm before we head back for supper?"

"That sounds lovely. What about the... panther?"

"Michael and Nicholai will happily take care of it. They'll carry him off and have his pelt cleaned and shown off in one of their homes. I'd rather not listen to them bicker about who gets to keep the animal anyway."

"Do you not want the pelt?" My shoulders fall away from my ears.

"No." He laughs. "What am I going to do with it? We've got enough rugs."

"Oh."

The line of trees starts to thin and I can see the break of the canopy allowing the sun to shine freely not too far ahead. The noise of the forest has returned with the panther's death. A delicate wind cools my sheen of sweat.

"So tell me about yourself, Briar Anders." Kai smiles over my shoulder. "It seems my brother's gotten to know you but now you're with me and there isn't much more to you than the fact that you prefer jeans to dresses and are impeccably mortal."

I send him a wary glance. What is there to say? What would he even care to know?

"What do you want to know?"

"What was your home like in the mortal world?" His tone is sincerely curious.

"I lived in an apartment. It was small, kind of falling apart, but it was mine which was all that mattered."

"An apartment?"

"It's a large building with separate living spaces that contain a bedroom, bathroom, kitchen, and living area. Multiple families or people share the entire building."

"Like an Inn?" Kai offers, grasping at the forgotten bits of the human world. "It truly has been far too long since I've ventured into the mortal realm. It's probably much different than I remember it."

"Like an Inn except you don't rent the room for a night, you live there. And the space is much larger." I pause. "Lincoln thought the same thing. Why don't you visit the mortal world often? Is it because there is no magic like there is here?"

"Ah, no, the lack of magic doesn't bother me. Humans can be quite fun." We break through the end of the forest, reappearing in the long valley. "It's more so that there are many realms that can be visited. I have others that are more cherished or favored."

"H-how many are there?"

"Quite a few actually." He chews on his lip. "There is this realm that is pretty strictly filled with Trolls. They make the best food. Amazing dining. Then there is another realm that is more a hodgepodge of species, but their technology is... advanced. It confuses me, but it's very intriguing and fun."

"You don't worry about these other realms?"

"Why would I?"

"What if there was a war between them?"

"Most realms are blissfully unaware of the others. Ours is one of the few that actually allows crossover, which is why we have Shadow Fae. Though you have to be careful when you're traveling around. Portals exist that take you to the Lost Realm, where no portals exist to take you back."

My nose crinkles as I toss him a dubious look over my shoulder. "There has to be a portal to take you back."

"How?" Kai chuckles.

"How else would you even know about the Lost Realm?"

His body freezes as he churns over the thought. His eyes glaze over and he looks off into the distance. "Never thought of it that way. But I'd assume a seer somewhere is how we know."

I shrug. *I'm not the expert on Fae realms.*

47

The horse walks calmly to the back of the castle. I eye the many balconies that protrude from dark stone walls. Behind it's plain, not-particularly-welcoming front half, is a much more appealing backyard. The back of the castle has one long balcony, I can only assume belongs to the King and Queen, then below it, hedges pathed in a knee height maze. Blue flowers poke off the bushes. Their sweet scent fills the air. Honestly, I'm surprised when I can't find any traces of a Reminints tree.

"Where is *your* Reminint's tree?"

I watch the maze with interest, admiring small statues of what I'd call cherubs but their ears come to a point and their mouths are open to reveal shark-like teeth. Whatever they are, perhaps I don't want to go to their realm.

"Reminint's is a drug that has been banned in the Iron Court." His voice is rough.

"Oh is it?" I scoff.

"Yes, well sometimes it pays to be the prince. Fae tend to turn their heads from my less than respectable actions."

An array of trees, filled with colorful fruits, zigzags through the yard beyond the maze. We trot along through them. I breeze in the citrus, my stomach growling.

Kai doesn't seem to mind the silence when it does settle between us. I wonder if it's because he was raised to show a level of respect to others, whomever he's deemed his peers like a mortal queen. I'm quite content letting the sun warm my cheeks, though his oversized jacket still hangs on me making my body warm faster.

I stay quiet as we round the castle again. A door is propped open with a few servants chatting on the few steps that lead inside. As they see their prince, they quiet and bow. His arms pull gently at the reins slowing the stallion to a stop. He drops from the horse. His boots meet the grass with a quiet thud and he lifts his arms to me.

Both servants watch with piqued interest as I let him wrap his hands around my waist and lower me to the ground as if I weighed nothing more than a penny.

Honestly, the fact that someone can be strong enough to move me without effort is mildly attractive.

"May I?" Kai offers his elbow. It's then that I notice the baldric on his chest is empty.

"You left your short sword in the panther."

"Ah, the Dukes will be kind enough to return it, I'm sure."

I smile at the servants, pulling down the skirt of the dress. As if that does a lick of good. God above, what have I gotten myself into?

Arm in arm, we enter the castle. The door leads us into the kitchens, where staff are busily preparing the meal. Servants bow as they catch the prince in passing. Their eyes quickly shift and linger on me.

"How often do you bring guests home?"

"Not often." He reaches for another door. "I think my

last guest was, perhaps, somewhere in the range of one hundred to two hundred years ago."

I have to pause long enough to totally register if I've shit my pants or not. The lifespan of the Fae is almost unfathomable. And it's no wonder I'm gaining attention from others if Kai doesn't make a habit of bringing lovers home.

"And... how old are you?"

"Does the age difference scare you?" He smoothly avoids the question.

The door opens into a large dining room with purple velvet wallpaper clinging everywhere the eye can see. The room would feel dark if it wasn't for the line of chandeliers above the long metal table. Rowan is leaned back in a seat, his dusty boot resting on the table's edge. Violet lounges in a much more proper way, admiring the length of her nails.

"Sneaking through the servant's entrance?" Rowan picks at his teeth.

"It's appalling that your nasty shoes are resting where we eat." Kai retorts. Slipping his arm from mine, he grips a sleek metal chair and pulls it away from the table for me. "Please, sit."

"I see the outfit is holding up well." Violet grins.

I try not to give myself a once over to make sure I really am put together. After that high-speed chase through the woods I feel like the dress should be in shreds. Kai's jacket does well enough to keep me covered.

"I'm mildly annoyed," she continues, "that my brother hasn't tried to take it off yet."

Kai sighs loudly, retreating to the seat next to mine. "If I remember correctly, Briar is exclusive."

Rowan snorts.

Violet's lip curls and she leans forward. "What?"

Right. Collin. No, that's not a thing anymore.

"Actually, I'm not anymore." I clear my throat.

"It never mattered to me anyway." Rowan shrugs.

"That's interesting." Violet looks between me and Kai, who folds his hands delicately in his lap holding her gaze unphased.

"Is it?" Kai finally responds.

"Yes."

I look between the three siblings who exchange gazes with one another in silent communication. Not one of them meets my eyes.

"So, er, has anyone heard what's happening in the Shadow Court? Surely, Cordelia will have shit a brick by now?" Anything to pull the awkward attention from me.

"Oh, she's pissed. As far as I've been told she nearly set half her ballroom on fire when she realized. Though, I think Lincoln jumped the gun—that's a human phrase, right? —on escorting you out of the court because word is that the seer she found has a lot of travelling to do before they make it to her court to do her dirty work," Kai answers.

The kitchen doors we entered swing open and servants wander in with steaming plates, setting the meals down in front of each of us. I do my best to smile at the servant who watches me with blatant curiosity. With my mumble of 'thank you', they retreat back to the stoves.

"I'm surprised Lincoln hasn't told you." Violet picks up her fork, spearing a few vegetables on the end.

Kai and Rowan also dig into their meals. Though my stomach rumbles, I stare down at the food for a minute thinking.

"No, he's been... busy, I guess."

"Can't you just look into his thoughts? Didn't he open his mind to you? Why else did Kai get the ever-loving shit beat out of him when he took Linc's punishment?" she continues.

He what now?

The air between us feels fragile. I'm certain if I take too deep of a breath or move too quickly I'll be ignored or my questions will be shot down. Still, I rotate to give Kai my full attention. His cheeks heat but he faces his plate without acknowledging how heavily my attention burns into him.

"You took Lincoln's punishment for protecting my thoughts?" I whisper.

His fork clatters against his plate as he drops it and frowns at Violet. She smiles sweetly back at him.

"Lincoln needed to be with you. There wasn't time for him to be punished and heal and be back doing what he needed to. Plus, I'm the heir. My punishments are swifter and less public. It was a quick lashing and I was fine. I'm fine." His eyes shine like the fiery stars above.

"Wow, I'm just surprised." I turn back, finally grabbing my silverware. "I thought you all thought so little of Lincoln you'd let him fight on his own."

"Oh, we love Linc, but he is, undoubtedly, less than. Kai didn't do it for Lincoln's sake. He did it for yours." Rowan chews as he talks, pointing his fork at me. "If Lincoln was beat bad enough, he wouldn't be able to protect you."

"I liked it better when I thought you were doing it for your brother." I sigh.

Some things, like this realm's view on Shadow Fae, cannot be changed in a day. It would take work, years of trying to shift their societal norms, for it to be understood that they were all equal. I've learned enough from the human world to know that if you value one race, one religion, one sexuality, one...whatever that makes someone different than you, less than your own, it makes the world sticky with hate. Humans hating humans only brings war and heartache. Such as, Fae hating Fae will one day prove to have a breaking point here.

"Lincoln doesn't need me to fight his battles." Kai cuts into the chunk of meat on his plate. "But you... you may need some help."

His words settle heavy on my shoulders. He's right, after all. I'm weaker than the Fae here. I'm a foreigner to their culture and traditions.

Every bite turns to stone as it hits my stomach. Something has to be done. I can't just keep letting them fight my battles for me. I think about my necklace, hidden in Kai's guest room.

I need my powers. Whatever part of me has been suppressed or taken away or whatever it is, I can't survive without them anymore.

Mortal, no more.

Shadow Fae blood belongs to me.

I'M NOT HIGH, YOU ARE

DINNER CONTINUES WITH LITTLE CONVERSATION. Rowan ponders how such a delicate flower like myself could possibly enjoy hunting. Kai remains gentlemanly and refrains from giving him the full details of my unbridled fear in the given situation. Though we both laugh as I try to explain that cats in the human world do not get that big.

Rowan watches us with focused attention as I catch myself touching Kai's shoulder. Throwing my head back with a hearty chuckle. It's funnier looking back on it now than it was in the actual moment.

Afterwards, I'm escorted back to my room where I find myself with a full closet and a crashing wave of exhaustion. Sleep beckons me and I succumb to it until dawn creeps through my windows and a servant enters my room with a full tray of food.

Breakfast sits in my lap while I blink away my

dreams. An arrangement of sweets, mostly comparable to donuts or pastries are stacked into a small mountain of food. I skip the sweets in favor of the dark roast coffee steaming in a mug. Nothing like a hit of caffeine to prepare me for whatever the Iron Court has in store for me. I watch the door waiting for any one of the royals to burst in without knocking, but I get to finish the breakfast in peace.

There is even time for me to stand and look out the window. Unlike Lincoln's room in the Shadow Court, there is no view of the city. My guest suite looks out at the valley, slick with morning dew, that Kai and I had ridden through yesterday. Winds blow the tree limbs of the forest at the valley's edge. How many other beasts live within it as wild as the white panther? How deadly would a walk through the woods be for someone like me?

The thoughts only grow my need to release my power. I step down into the living area, a fire burns in the hearth, though I haven't a clue when it was started or by whom. On the mantle is an arrangement of décor, fresh flowers, a small canvas painting, and an assortment of porcelain vases. My fingers grip the cool, smooth, lid of a cream-colored pot that reminds me of what someone would keep sugar in for tea. Quickly, not trusting that I'm not watched, I chance a glance inside. The large ruby pendant rests at its bottom, the dark chain curled in a pile on top of it. It shimmers the longer I watch. Power. This is my power. Careful not to hurt what must be very expensive pieces, I set the lid back down.

Warmth from the fire heats my legs. I hold my palms forward long enough to gather the warmth on my hands before turning for the closet. The once empty metal bars are now filled with an assortment of gowns. More than I remember either Rowan or Violet picking. After some consideration, I opt for a soft yellow gown that dips half way down my stomach with panels of material that come to my ankles. Slits run the length of the skirt over and over again, so much so that the skirt itself is just a long fringe. This, though, feels safer than what they had me in yesterday. Even if every step reveals the entirety of my legs at least my vagina isn't hanging out. That has to count for something, it does in my book.

The pointed pink heels that provide a stark contrast to my dress, click as I move toward the door. It's a confident feeling, like I'm playing dress up, but I love that it consumes me. It's an improvement from yesterday's self-conscious state.

I step out into the hallway, jumping with a start as I realize Rowan is leaned up against the wall. He stands ignoring my choking gasp.

"Ready for this tour?"

I'd forgotten about that, but I guess I'm technically ready. What else am I going to do with my day?

"The answer to that will be determined once you tell me how long you've been lurking outside my door for?"

"Long enough, but not too long." Rowan pushes his long braids over the back of his shoulder, strolling forward down the hall.

I step lightly to follow. "That's vague."

"It's meant to be."

He hovers near me, his arm brushing mine as we walk. We stroll in silence as he takes me to the main entrance of the castle. As we reach the large doors, he claps his hands.

"So, clearly. This is our entryway."

"Yes, I recognized the long, long hallway that leads.... To nothing." I sigh. "Can you explain to me why every hall looks too similar to the last? Could your interior designer not be bothered to come up with anything else?"

"Eh, it's meant to be that way. It's confusing for guests but it's also confusing for intruders. Come on." He laces his fingers with mine.

I'm tempted to refuse or at the very least make mention of the intimate touching, but he's already pulling me ahead with excitement. His boots slap loudly against the floor.

"Think of it like this," he says, "The outermost halls," he points down the halls branching first from the entryway, "are offices, storage, some of Violet's extensions of her own closet, and other pretty boring things. So the first two halls in the front and the first two halls in the back are boring nothings, pretty well. The longer we go," he keeps dragging me forward. "The more interesting it gets."

"How many halls are there in total through the castle?"

"Ten-ish."

"Ish? How can there be an... ish hallway?"

Rowan laughs. Internally, I'm making notes to remember what sort of halls are what. As Rowan has described them, halls one and two, as well as ten and nine are... offices 'and other boring things.'

"The next set of halls are bedchambers. Guest suites mainly on the first floor. Your suite is down that hall. If you follow the stairs," He points to the rising steps a few beats ahead, "then on the next floor you'll find the royal's bedchambers."

Rowan pauses at the foot of the stairs. He lifts his free hand to stroke the knuckle of his pointer finger down the curve of my face. "My room is the second door on the left."

I exhale loudly through my nose and push his hand away. Holding up our interlacing fingers, I raise my brows with question. His knowing smirk only grows before he tugs me forward again. With loud clicking steps, I try to keep pace.

Halls one, two, ten, and nine are boring things. Halls three four, eight, seven, are bedchambers. What's left? The middlemost halls? Halls number five and six.

"I have a guess as to what is in the middle." I say to Rowan's broad shoulders.

"Yes, you've probably guessed it."

"Dining, banquet halls, and ballrooms?" I mimic Rowan's pleasant accent.

"I do not sound like that." He pauses as we reach the middle of the castle.

"Yes, you do."

The frown that formed on his lips only intensifies as he takes offense. "You must be bad at doing impressions. Do Lincoln's." He demands.

"Fine." I've got nothing to prove but I'll be damned if I'm not great at impressions. I square my shoulders and stand as tall as I can manage, holding my chin perfectly straight, and puffing my chest. "Your curiosity is troublesome, Briar. Let me fetch you some other things to intrigue it." I give it the same roll of the accent as all the Iron Court seems to share.

"Damn that was good. Do Kai."

Kai's easy. Proper but the relaxed version. I stand tall still but relax my chest and chin. I hold my hands lightly in front of me. Oh, and I can't forget the half-hooded eyes. "When the rains of life fall on the lakes of eternity the nearby city is less likely to run it dry."

"Ooo," Rowan bites his knuckle. "Spot on. Fuck, now I'm pissed because that *must* be what I sound like."

"Yeah, well." I shrug, careful of every step I take as I start back up. But I know everything else, it just repeats. "Where are we going now?"

"To the garden."

I don't remember seeing a garden when we passed the back on the castle on Kai's horse. It is not just the short hedge maze?

"Oh, is that near the back of the castle?"

"Yes, it's right out the back doors." He reaches for my

hand again. This time I notice how his thumb strokes against mine.

I'm slightly winded from our trip from the front of the castle all the way to the back. That's not even mentioning the way Rowan practically ran me through the tour. Does he have something else planned? God, I hope not.

"Where are your parents?" I ponder out loud. I've yet to see the infamous king and queen since my arrival. Though that's probably a good thing because playing the part of Kai's lover doesn't entirely sound exciting.

"Busy." He shrugs.

"But they're here?"

"Oh, yes."

He pushes open the door that shields us from the outside world. Finally. The fresh air fills our lungs as we step out. As expected, the lush leaves of the small hedges that create the maze-like patio hit us about midcalf. The greens are rich with the life that grows here, vibrant and thriving.

Rowan leans down, twisting a plump berry from its hedge and tosses it into his mouth. He hums an appreciation. All along the bottom of the bushes, the sides that face inwards toward the castle, are different berries. Many of the small fruits grow next to the lovely indigo blooms I saw yesterday.

So there is a garden...at least Rowan wasn't trying to trick me into anything.

"I hear it's a custom in the mortal world for men to

give their partners flowers. Do you like flowers?" The Fae squats and teases his finger along the flowers.

Or maybe he is.

"I like flowers," I say cautiously.

"Then I'll pick some!"

"Well, it's only customary that I pick some for you too," I agree.

"It is? I don't remember hearing about that."

"Yes. It's a new trend. You go that way, I'll go this way and we'll meet in the middle with our bouquets."

No we won't. At least... I won't.

I look for taller well shaped hedges that I could slip behind. Or maybe I'll just round the corner and use the servants entrance again. Something tells me Rowan has way more planned than just picking flowers.

Rowan is already stepping over the ledge of green and onto the next path. He's selective as he looks at the variety of blooms. Thinking much too hard on what I'd like or not like. It makes me almost sad that I'm about to run and hide from him. Maybe I should just tell him I'm not interested. Well, I mean... I pretty well have.

I keep my eyes trained on him, pretending to have interest in picking flowers for him in return, until he's far enough away that I shoulder myself behind the oval shaped bush that covers my height even in these heels. Along the back side of the castle wall there's another door that leads out to this small garden. I give the Fae one last look before I dart to it.

"This might be the biggest bouquet you've ever received." Rowan laughs from the distance.

I hold the knob. "It's not a competition!"

"Actually, that's exactly what it is." Rowan says, though I hardly catch the words.

Swiftly, I close the door and start moving down the hall. The child-like fear that arises in any good hide and seek game fills me now. The adrenaline of getting caught in my act of sneaking off. Maybe it's more comparable to skipping class in high school. I don't want to be enrolled in the Science of Rowan Ziko. I'm still trying to learn the History of Lincoln Ziko.

Damn, I'm nothing if not devoted.

Maybe that was my problem with Collin. Maybe this space between me and Lincoln is a good thing. This way we can't rush into anything. Not that he seems all that ready to do that anyway...

Footsteps echo behind me. I can't turn to see who it is. My fear won't let me. Instead I do an even more dangerous thing and throw myself into the nearest room and slam the door closed.

Papers shift from under Kai's boots as he pulls his feet from his desk. His eyes are red and his head snaps up from its reclined position on his chair. Quickly, I recognized the room as his office.

"You look hard at work." I press my ear to the door.

"Sorry, stressful morning." He rubs at his eyes.

"I see." I wait for the sound of thundering boots to

follow me in. Steps go by, but they are too gentle to be Rowan.

"Do you, uh, need something?"

"What?" I lift my ear from the door for a moment to allow my brain a second to take in what he's saying. "No, no I'm fine."

"Then what are you doing here?"

I blink. Smoothing down the fray of the skirt that's pushed back behind me in the whirlwind of movement from ushering myself in, I plaster on a soft smile. "Hiding."

"It's Rowan, isn't it?" Kai frowns. His eyes are hardly even open as he watches me.

"He's persistent."

"You say that like it's a good thing." Kai tilts his chair back again, resting his hands on his chest. It's a pose that suggests he could lull himself to sleep rather quickly.

"It is a good thing, just not in this particular scenario."

Two empty chairs wait in front of his desk, plush and inviting. I shift my gaze to them before escorting myself forward. The fabric is velvety, reminiscent of the dining chairs. It brushes against my skin in a comforting way, a warm way. Kai's office actually has a chill to it. I'd assumed it was the tiny article of clothing I wore last time I was here. Though... I guess this one isn't much better.

"Would you like me to talk to him?" Kai's voice is dull, but he arches a brow.

"Would you?" I try not to gush. "I mean, if you could."

"Or you could tell him yourself."

I frown at his suggestion.

"I have. I've told him I'm not interested."

"Perhaps he is just confused then by your mixed signals."

My jaw drops open. My mixed signals? Do these Fae think I've done anything to lead Rowan on? No. Not a chance.

"Mixed signals?" I finally force myself to regain my composure.

"You kissed him. At the Lavender Lounge if I'm correct." Kai tries to blink his eyes open to really look at me.

"I was high."

"Do you often make it a habit of kissing men you don't like when you're high?"

What sort of question is that? My hands curl into fists. Heat rises to a blush that creeps up my neck.

"I was. I am in a confusing time. Collin and I broke up. I've been thrown into this new realm with... with *magic*. It's a lot to process."

"Damn. Maybe you should be getting high." He shrugs, saying it as a joke. Yet, my gaze still drifts to his jacket where I know his bottle of Reminints waits. "Do you... want some?" His words are slow and drawn out.

"No." I wave my hand and look off at his bookshelf littered with knick knacks. But my attention drifts back to it. I could use a moment to just relax. And Jase suggested it was comparable to alcohol once and I'm not an alcoholic so this... this should be *safe*. "Maybe."

"Oh, Briar Anders. How scandalous," he gasps, but the dramatics are muted by his drugs. He slips his hand into his jacket and pulls out the small vile. "Just a few. Then no more for you, light weight."

"Do not tell anyone... anyone that I did this."

"Secrets safe with me, dear." His cheeky grin does little to give me confidence.

"Promise." I hold a hand out for him to drop a few sparkling petals into.

"Promise," he repeats, extending the bottle toward me. "Wait, you're not going to try and kiss me when you get high, are you?" He pulls the bottle back with a laugh.

"Not a chance."

"Wow, maybe don't say it with such certainty next time." He shakes some petals out.

They fall softly into my palm. I'm still, watching them glitter from the light that covers us. Am I really about to get high with the Prince of the Iron Court? Yes. And I think Lincoln would want me to. They all harped on it often enough when I was in the Shadow Court, that I needed to relax, to release all my pent-up energy. Well this isn't sex but it's as good as it's going to get. Before I let myself think any harder on the subject, I place both petals on my tongue. They melt like a chocolate, dissolving in the sweet sensation of static against my cheeks.

Reminints are a curious thing. So delicate. So delicious. So... relaxing. My posture, most immediately, slumps into the chair. I let out a long breath.

"Now, don't you feel better." Kai closes his eyes, resuming his position with his feet propped on the desk.

"These are fast acting." My eyes flutter close.

Before where the room felt suffocatingly small, the walls always pressing in on me no matter how large the room physically is, now it's like a swimming pool. The hairs on my arms rise. My limbs are light, swimming in the air where I can feel every shifting wind created by the large ceiling fan above us. I'd say half my body is numb, that near unmovable feeling, but I'm aware of everything. I just no longer care.

Kai and I sit quietly together, letting minutes, possibly hours, move by us without a worry. Somewhere in the back of my mind I wonder if Rowan will come looking for me. If he'll be pissed when he finds me. Yet, those thoughts are too far away from me to actually grasp. Not that I even want to think about them. So I let them drift off.

My lips buzz with a smile as I picture Lincoln and the exited but guarded smile he'd give me if he saw me in this state. We could have a lot of fun together with some Remininats. He'd probably remind me I'm a queen and there are better things I should be doing with my time. Maybe I do understand Kai's addiction.

"You know," I start, "Everyone keeps telling me I'm a queen. I'm *the* queen."

"Mmhmm."

Neither of us open our eyes. I snuggle lower into the chair.

"But, like, I don't feel like a queen."

"You weren't raised," he pauses, "with the idea that you're to be looked up to." His words are sluggish, and said with every effort to produce a coherent thought. "So I could see how... odd it would be to all of a sudden be getting pushed into leadership."

"It's not that." My head lulls to the side. *I could take a nap right now. Maybe I will. I'm sure Kai would like a nap.*

"No?"

Both brows rise as I try to remember where this conversation was going and what exactly I had said. My thoughts echo a jumble of our dialogue back to myself.

"...no." I clear my throat. "Aren't I supposed to be powerful? My dad was Fae, yet I'm so... so...so very human."

"You're high right now." Kai laughs.

I can't help but chuckle too. "So are you."

Our laughs settle comfortably between us. So much so I consider my nap again. But a nagging need still whispers back to me.

"Kai, I have a necklace."

"Mmm, did Violet pick it out for you? You didn't really seem like the excessive jewelry type so I didn't bother asking for an arrangement for you."

"No. I brought it with me from the Shadow Court."

The prince shifts. My eyelids flutter open to find him watching me with mild interest. The pink in the whites of his eyes has faded but not by much.

"Is it from Lincoln?"

"Ah, Lincoln doesn't seem like the romantic gesture type."

Kai scratches at his head, letting his arm fall with a loud thump against the arm of his chair. "You'd be surprised. Though it'd be awfully daring of him to give someone like you a gift like that."

Maybe I want Lincoln to be daring like that. Maybe I want there to be a little spark of fire in his veins that fights for me. For us.

"It's from my aunt, Jase's mother." Even with the effects of the calming drugs I feel my pulse pick up at the thought of it. Without the Reminints I imagine I'd be light headed or sick to my stomach with anxiety. Lincoln told me not to tell a soul, not to let anyone get their hands on it. "I think, I think it contains my powers." I finally admit.

"Oh."

"Lincoln said so."

"Lincoln is... smart enough to know so." Kai folds his hands into his lap, his attention never falling away from me.

"Do you know how I can get my powers? How can I become like you?"

"Yes, um, items like that." He chews on his lip. "That's a good question." Kai shakes his head. "Um, you need a powerful seer to help you unlock them. I can pull some strings for you."

"You're doing me all the favors today, huh?" I give him a faint smile.

"Well, it's the least I could do for my royal guest." He nods his head.

"Do you feel like you could fall asleep right now?" I yawn, stretching my arms above my head, careful to watch my chest so that my boobs don't lift right out of the gown. Strips of fabric have fallen off my thighs, leaving my legs exposed.

"I'm on my way off the Remininats, I don't think I could nap now if I wanted."

"How sad," I practically purr. Kai had put my worries to ease so quickly. The prince is nothing if not accommodating and gentlemanly.

Just as I let my eyes close once more the door bursts open with a gush of air. Rowan cocks his head looking from me to his brother, a large bundle of flowers, perfectly arranged, clutched between both hands. Kai looks from me to his sibling, pursing his lips.

"Rowan, hi." I wave.

"I'm not high. You are." Rowan accuses.

I start to feign offense, my hand rising to touch my collar bone. As I frown, my lips fight the urge to point upward and a sputtering laugh rolls out of me. "I'm sorry. I got distracted."

Kai stands, straightening his clothes and walks with a confidence only the heir to the throne could possess. He leans forward, pushing his nose into the bouquet and breathes them in.

"For me." Kai starts to take the flowers.

"No, actu—"

"For me." He says more firmly, scooping them out of Rowan's hands and clutching them close to his chest.

Rowan's gaze is wide with anger. He recovers quickly, forcing his hands into his jacket and leaning against the door frame. "Guess I'll have to pick you another one, love."

"Another one for me, you mean." Kai raises his eyebrows.

"No, not you." Rowan says, confusion tinting his words.

I purse my lips at Kai's attempt at avoiding any uncomfortableness from Rowan's brash behavior.

"For me." He repeats once more. Kai digs his face into the petals, smelling their scent with great dramatics.

I cover my burning cheeks, trying to keep from giggling. But the drugs have done me no favors in being polite.

"Hurry off now," Kai urges his brother out the door. Rowan steps back, still scowling. The prince closes the door, with Rowan on the other side turning back to me. "After all this... you're going to owe me."

Then we both dissolve into a fit of laughter.

VOTE BRIAR ANDERS

Lunch passes with little to no notice of Kai and I. At some point his work began again and I curl into his chair, just watching. Occasionally, he looks up to catch my gaze and flash me a fleeting smile.

I lose track of time, sitting in an upright fetal position just admiring my friend. When dinner comes around, he gently shakes my shoulders, pulling me from the nap I'd eventually fallen into. Kai helps hold me upright even now. Waking up from a drugged sleep is hard.

One arm is looped around my waist. He's holding me firmly but also allowing as much distance between as the position will allow.

"By the time we reach the dining hall, you'll feel fine. It just takes a minute to re-adjust. You were sleeping rather heavy."

I scrunch my nose. "Yeah, I'm okay. I'm fine." Carefully, I push off of him and teeter on my heels.

"You sure?"

Finding my balance, I smile. "Of course. I've got this."

He shrugs, clasping both hands behind his back as he watches me. Honestly, I think I'm doing rather well. My heels click with a steady rhythm as we move together toward the dining room. Rowan's scowling face comes to mind.

"I hope Rowan isn't too bothered by us earlier."

"He's a grown ass man, he'll be fine. Don't worry about him."

"Okay." It's all I can do to nod because asking me not to worry is like asking the sun not to shine.

"So, not to sound like I'm prying." The Prince doesn't bother to smother the look of smugness as he practically skips forward. "but... is your apathy toward Rowan because you have interest elsewhere."

I scoff, cover my face with my hand. "Kai, now we sound like a couple of gossiping hens."

"What's wrong with that? I like talking with you. Gossip with me a little, Briar."

They all know it. I reassure myself. *Your attraction to Lincoln hasn't been hidden well. Might as well confess it.*

"I just don't want to lead him on, that's all." I try to say.

Kai rolls his eyes. "You're not fooling anyone."

"No?"

"No. I can tell you miss the half breed. It's a shame, because you could do better, you know?"

"Better than Lincoln?" I wish he were kidding, though I know he very much is not. "I'm half breed too, you know?"

"But you're a true royal one. A king's first born like myself. That's the difference" Kai brushes it off. "In a world where you were not a rightful Queen, I think Lincoln and you would likely be very nice together. Make beautiful babies."

I smile despite how much my stomach twists in silence.

The Prince continues, "You'll need a royal husband."

"Like you?" I deadpan.

Kai shifts, pointing his gaze off toward the ground. The door to the dining room is propped open, Rowan and Violet already in conversation as their voices drift to us. The smell of seasoned turkey greets me and my stomach twists with hunger.

"Yes but no. There are other courts to choose from. But I would be honored if you had any interest in me."

"Kai Ziko, are you blushing?" I laugh.

His eyes flair but more so as if he is addressing an internal dialogue rather than our conversation. His steps slow as we reach the dining hall.

"My parents have wanted to extend our reign and uniting two Courts would do just that. It's just a thought. Obviously, this isn't romantic." He raises his eyebrows as if to say, 'unless you want it to be'.

I swat at him. If I'd met Kai first would I still have fallen for Lincoln? Kai's patient and kind, but our relationship feels far too much like the stereotypical gay best friend scenario. Without the gay part, kind of.

"What about Jase? Are you guys... together?"

"Please, after you." He gestures for me to enter before him. "I'm not sure I would label it as officially together. Though I'd be inclined to invite him to stay at the castle much under the ruse you're playing."

The flash of the image of Jase goofily grinning in the handcuffs on the headboard of the bed comes to mind. I push the image off quickly wishing it had never come to mind.

"I'm sure he'd like that very much." I encourage. "But only if you promise not to break his heart."

"I'm a Prince, I can make no such promises." He winks, pulling out a chair for me to sit. His words don't settle well with me. He's playing the part of my friends' boyfriend who all too quickly gives me bad vibes. But I just can't help but like him because he is just so damn charming. Is it possible that Kai is too polite? Is that even a thing?

"I wouldn't sit there if I were you." Rowan wags a finger as I lower into my seat.

I still hover, just above the cushioned bottom. "Why not?"

"The King and Queen are joining us for dinner." Violet beams. She taps her long nails on the table's edge, looking eagerly between Kai and I. I wonder why she doesn't address them as Mother or Father.

"Well, shit," Kai sighs. "Come now." He hurriedly waves.

"This will be fun to watch." Rowan smirks from across the table.

Will it? A nervous energy builds inside of me only released in sweat that pools in my palms. I step around the chair allowing Kai to push it back in. He moves to his own seat, planting himself in it then points to his lap.

"Seriously?" I stare down at him.

"Oh, it's about to get really touchy feely and all sorts of creepy up in here." Violet leans forward.

"In front of your parents even?" My throat is itchy and dry. There's always a choice though, and I could choose not to. The consequences of that could be worse than what I'm prepared for.

It's only for a little bit, Briar. Kai is going to help you release your powers and after that you won't have to play this part anymore.

"Especially in front of our parents," Rowan answers.

"Fuck," I huff, lowering myself to perch on Kai's leg.

"I'm going to, uh, have to touch you." He crinkles his nose.

"Like, sexually?" The squeak in my voice is unattractive and makes it clear how utterly painful this plan of theirs really is.

"Yes, but not in the way you're thinking. Just like... touch you." His hands skim up my thighs. A long trail of goosebumps follows the caress.

I swallow, hard. My body responds with an unrequested urge, a wetness slick between my legs.

"Is that—" He starts to ask as we hear the approach of the King and Queen down the hall. Kai tilts his head up trying to talk over my shoulder. In a hushed voice he talks only to me. "It's going to be okay."

I'd heard those words too many times to count. This time I'm demanding more of myself. *Play the part. Play the part, Briar. Be the fucking human that's come because you're infatuated with Kai. With magic. With the Fae.*

I give him the slightest bob of my head, the smallest form of acknowledgment, before I lean into him. Kai's breathing hitches.

"I'm just saying, is all..." The king says as they round the corner.

"And I'll take that into consideration but there just isn't any reason—" The Queen stops, meeting my gaze with a frown. "Who is this?"

"Mother," Kai draws a hand up my arm. "This is Briar Anders. Isn't she pretty?" He tilts his face against my arm, inhaling loudly.

I smile, bringing my hand up to cup his face, then play through a few loose strands of hair. Her attention only narrows.

"Human." She spits. "Why did you bring it here? Why is it at my dinner table?"

She talks as if I'm a dog. Still, I try to look off into the distance and ignore her confrontation. Focusing solely on the smell that surrounds Kai. His sweet scent, always laced with a hint of Reminints.

Kai grabs my thighs. It's much more possessive than the gentle touch he'd given me before. His fingers dig into my skin, almost painfully, as he drags them up my legs, finally hovering at my inner thigh.

"I was bored and took a little trip to the Mortal Realm to remind me why what I do is so great. I found this little thing and she's very much impressed with us. Very playful too." He lifts one hand, grabs my face, and pinches my cheeks together. It takes all of me not to pull away. Pleasantly, I laugh at the gesture.

"Of course she is, son. She's a mortal." His father's lips are pursed. Did they tell the king of their plans for me in this court?

Servants usher themselves forward, pulling out seats for both the King and Queen. The Queen, with her black curls and pale toned skin, tosses her hair over her shoulder. She reminds me instantly of Lincoln. Their faces mirror one another. Though tall iron spikes rise off her scalp in thin, delicate pieces that interlock into her crown. One eye is the treasure color I'm fond of, the other totally grey. She looks anything but nice.

Holding her hands properly at her waist, she sits down careful not to wrinkle her deep violet gown that clings onto her curves. She allows her other children the smallest of glances.

The king holds a heavy stare with each one of them, a silent plea for answers and a vicious command to keep my title unknown, pushing his white blonde braid behind his back as he sits. The metal bands on his wrists clatter against his seat as he relaxes. Both Rowan and Violet have straightened in their chairs and their expressions have been wiped clean to indifference.

Kai's breath is hot on my skin. "It's all for good fun, Mother."

"Well, I'd hope so. She shouldn't even be eating with us." She hisses, unashamed that I can clearly hear everything she's saying.

I pout slightly, squirming in his lap. "I don't want to leave you." If she wants to treat me like a dog, I guess I can play the puppy.

"Would it serve you better if I took her to *eat* in her room?" Eat clearly doesn't mean *eat,* with the way he says it. Kai tilts his head into me.

"That would be rude." King Dravid says plainly, pushing back the black collared coat he wears.

"But I'm supposed to be subjected to eating with Kai's pet?" The Queen seethes.

Wow, this woman really is a piece of work.

I take a long slow breath, trying to focus on keeping my own emotions under control. My knuckles turn white as I fist my hands and Kai tenses as I lean into him stiffly.

"Just pretend she isn't there, dear." The king reaches for Queen Avaleen's hand, giving her a reassuring squeeze.

Kai slips a hand up to my waist, holding me steady, as I try to turn my gaze from the Queen and the King, with their demeaning view of humans and half-breeds. I focus my eyes on the dimly lit sconces or try to admire the velvet-like wallpapers. His hands are warm even through the materials of my dress, not like there truly is much.

"And how am I to be sure that this isn't that Mortal Queen Cordelia has lost her rocker over?"

Every heartbeat stops. Kai, Rowan, Violet, and I make no obvious moves or changes to our expressions but I can feel it as much as they can. A seed of worry lives in all of them.

Rowan spurts out a laugh, quickly followed by Violet's short chortle.

"The who now?" Kai leans forward, tilting me with his body.

A new sheen of sweat clings to me. All I can do is pray Avaleen can't smell my fear in the air.

"Mortal. Queen." Her lips press in a firm line as her children poke fun at her idea. The laughter quickly dies.

"No Queen, but I bet she would love that." Kai draws a hand down my cheek, forcing my gaze to him. His intense gaze focuses on me with a plea to play along. "Isn't that right, Cupcake?"

My tongue feels too heavy for words. My mouth too dry.

"Can't I just marry you and become a queen?" I whisper back.

"For the love of all things good," The Queen drops her hands dramatically into her lap. "Now she really thinks she can marry you?"

I channel my measly acting skills into confusion then sadness. "What does she mean?"

"Nothing, nothing." Kai brushes it off. "Mother quit trying to ruin my fun."

Avaleen opens her mouth to speak, but the doors to the kitchen quickly open and a slew of servants scuttle around us dropping fresh plates and large glasses of wine in front of us. Some sort of chicken, maybe? Broccoli and a cheesy pasta.

Dinner continues with many side-eyed glances. I try to eat in the perched position on Kai's lap. My plate sits next to Kai's in the same space as we shared currently. The moment I make a move to go back to a single seat, Kai clamps a hand on my waist and whispers, "Why would you want to be anywhere else, Cupcake?"

So I eat with my elbows oddly high so I continuously get in Kai's way or hit him accidentally. My back aches as I have to hunch to cut apart my food. Kai snaps his fingers and a servant rushes forward and cuts his plate for him. What is he a child? I shift and remember his other hand on my waist.

The meal concludes as the Queen gives her children one final look. Her silverware hits her plate with an announcing *thwack*. "As usual, it was lovely to see you. I'll make arrangements to meet with each one of you this week."

The king, not yet finished with his plate, scoots himself out of his chair and stands to pull Avaleen's out.

When she holds her skirts and heads toward the door, he follows.

"Oh, and Kai," She stops at the door. "Maybe keep your pets confined to your room next time."

The moment her back turns to us, Rowan lifts his hand. He points an indifferent finger at a servant and gestures toward the door. "Could you just close that for us." All the while, my mouth has surely hit the floor.

Both King Dravid and Queen Avaleen resume their chatter down the hall but their words are lost to us as the doors click shut. Rowan growls under his breath, both hands on the table as he stretches into his chair. Violet wilts into her seat, as theatrically as possible. Kai's head tilts until his blonde ponytail is ruffled against the chair at such an angle he's exposing his throat to me.

"That was so *painful!*" Violet cries.

"Is it like this every time?" I finally close my gaping mouth.

"Yes." Rowan and Kai groan in unison.

"And she's making *appointments* with us now." Rowan uses his first two fingers to make air quotes as he talks. "Who makes appointments with their own children?"

Kai's eyes are closed again and I'm certain it's because his parents have utterly exhausted him. Is this what Lincoln had to grow up with? Did his mother even let him dine with them? If so, was she this obnoxiously rude?

Watching the servants slowly make their way back

into the kitchen, I stand. A lazy groan leaves me as I push against my back.

"Mother makes appointments with each of us regularly. It's our allotted time with her. At this age it's mainly to make sure we are upholding our duties and protecting our image. When we were younger it was chit-chat while she helped teach us to do simple magic or something else of that nature. Once, she taught me to embroider." Violet sticks her tongue out. "What a wasted talent I now have."

"If only we could all be so lucky. She tried to teach me to play the piano." Kai finally lifts his head.

"Tried?" I offer. I grab my plate and move to the seat I'd originally occupied. Most of my meal was uneaten. It's hard to have enough oomph to cut your food when you're sitting like a dummy in a ventriloquist's lap.

"Oh, I know how to play. But my fingers are a bit clumsy." Kai wiggles his ringed fingers before picking up his fork to eat his meal too.

I shove a piece of chicken into my mouth and try not to think about his fingers on my bare skin. Both Rowan and Violet push their empty plates away. They had plenty of opportunity to finish in the lingering silence their parents offered.

"I thought you told me she liked humans."

"Seems she wasn't in a particularly good mood today." Violet rolls her eyes. "It's hit or miss with her.

"You two played your part well." Rowan smirks. "If I didn't know any better, I'd assume that chemistry was real."

"You are just jealous," Kai says between bites. "You wish Briar could be a pretty object on your lap."

Rowan chuckles. "You're not wrong. Nothing you said there was a lie."

"Just don't get your hopes up, brother." Violet picks at her teeth.

"I think it's too late for that," Kai interjects before Rowan can speak. They exchange bickersome expressions.

The room without the king and queen feels less stuffy. My shoulders still hurt from the constant tension they had held during the meal. As I'm finishing my plate, I find myself looking absently at the king's plate, still plenty full.

It's clear who the powerhouse is in this kingdom. Queen Avaleen has everyone pinched and until I get my powers and claim my crown, I'll be just another thing for her to crush under her shining, pointed-toed heels.

I think this realm could use a taste of a queen that isn't wicked.

Not that I'm saying that Avaleen is comparable to Cordelia... because like... she isn't. Avaleen wasn't a ruthless madwoman for one.

But the standards of this realm need reform.

And I'm the right woman for the job.

Vote Briar Anders.

SLIPPERY SLOPE

THE UNCOMFORTABLE SILENCE from dinner follows Kai and I down the halls. While every passing hall resembles both the one before and the one after it, thanks to Rowan's quick guided tour, I now have some sense of where I'm going.

Seeing as my dress doesn't have pockets, the greatest downfall and most certainly an engineered feat of a misogynistic culture, I find my hands feeling lost. I try to let my arms swing at my sides but it feels too forced for the pace Kai has set next to me. Yet, if I clasp my hands in front of me not only do I become some innocent character from the eighteen-hundreds, but my interlaced fingers bounce against my stomach, now bloated from eating. There is clearly no winning with Fae fashion.

Kai's hands, I note, are clasped behind his back. He whistles softly as he escorts me to my room. Oblivious to my nervous state.

"Kai?" I finally break the quiet.

In front of us, two servants pull the curtains of the balcony closed. The sun sets without the vivid pinks and oranges as if it too is exhausted by today.

"Yes?" He lifts a brow, his whistle dead on his lips.

"Your mother is awful."

His chin drops to the floor as he stifles his laugh. "And?"

"And I don't think I can wait to release my powers. Some things need to change. In the Shadow Court... and here."

"Even if you are a queen, Briar, you have no reign over the Iron Court," he reminds me carefully.

"But as a queen I'll finally have a voice. I can help Fae. Plus, one day you'll have the throne." I smile, gently. "And you are ready for change, right?"

"Hmm, I'm not sure I'm going to be the king you think I'll be."

"It's the queen who holds the power here, isn't it?" Our steps slow as we reach my door. We face each other but neither of us moves for the knob.

"And I'm just the pretty little side piece." Kai returns my grin but something dark burns in his gaze.

There is pity in my heart for Kai, at the way that he views his own role. He has power, but he's helpless.

"Who are you going to marry?" I settle with crossing my arms over my chest, in the way that hides my breasts instead of putting them on display.

"Well, there are other Fae Courts with Princesses

with who would probably love to rule. I'm sure my Mother will make arrangements for our Courtship if her current plan falls through." He drops his gaze.

"...Current plan?"

"She wants to make a deal with Cordelia since Lincoln is nothing more to her than a soldier."

"It's never good to make deals with the devil." I laugh to cover up my rising anxiety.

"Yes, well, deals between one devil and another aren't often questioned." He swallows. "My mother is writing up a proposal for Cordelia and I's marriage. In exchange, our Courts will be merged into one with our reigns becoming equal. I'm the first born, but I'm also a male therefore the power in my court defaults to whomever I marry. My mother would like to ensure that our family remains in power... and expanding our court is an additional plus."

"You can't marry Cordelia." I hold myself tighter.

"It's not ideal." Kai agrees, leaning toward me to finally open the door. "But if you become queen, it won't have to be a worry. Right?" His voice is strained.

"Right," I say slowly, trying to process.

I don't have parents to rule over me, to guide me in decisions. Who will I marry? More worrisome, who will they expect me to marry? My mind wanders to Lincoln, but our relationship is too new to consider marriage.

"Will I have a, uh, counsel or something?"

"Yes, they will probably talk you through your

options." Kai looks inside my room, waiting for me to enter first.

My feet remain firmly planted. "If I'm the queen will I have a choice in who I marry?"

"Are we talking about my brother? The lesser, but much more withstandable, one?"

"Yes, but no. Maybe. I'm not sure." My words trip over themselves, stumbling from my lips in an embarrassing stutter that makes Kai genuinely smile.

"That's between you and your counsel," he amends, with a sigh. Dragging a hand down his face, he motions with the other for me to go inside.

I shake my head. His smile quickly falters.

"Is something wrong?"

"I want to see a seer. Tomorrow." It's the first confident, and if I do say so myself, queenly command I've given. Though, I imagine a prince has little want to be commanded.

"Tomorrow?"

I nod.

Kai lets go of a long breath, looking me up and down. "Are you sure the Reminints aren't still affecting you?"

"I'm fairly certain."

"That's enough for me." His hands disappear behind his back, again. "I think I know of a seer we can go to that can help. It's a rather hard and long trip for a human. Pack up a bag and I'll make arrangements for tomorrow. Will that satisfy you?"

"It very much will."

Kai bows. He takes my hand, flipping it, and presses a kiss to my palm the way he's always done. Always so proper.

"Kai, are we friends?" *Wow, Briar. What a fucking awkward way to say that.*

"I like to think so."

I take a step closer to him. He leans away but doesn't move from where he stands. His lips tilt slightly into a frown. The smell of Reminints clings to his clothes, and his breath.

This court, though they haven't left me alone except to get some sleep, has felt lonely. Lincoln hasn't been here and while I'm sure Rowan would take me up on the offer, I need some form of contact. A hug. I just want a hug.

Trying to force every ounce of my stiff, gracelessness, I rush to close the space between us. I bury my face in the finery of his suit, weaving my hands under his arms, and fasten my grip around the hard, lean muscle he is built out of.

Kai feels like an immovable prop for the entirety of a minute. His words fan my hair onto my forehead as he talks against my head. "I've been awfully polite. I've tried very, very hard to keep some sort of space for you since you were not raised in our ways. You were exclusive, now you're not. I, uh, understand this is by no means sexual or romantic, but I'm ecstatic that you're doing it." He melts over me. One arm winds over my back, the other presses my head against him, tucking it under his chin. We stand like this, soaking up each other.

As time passes our breathing synchronizes. Every heartbeat is shared. My warmth becomes his warmth and his mine, seeping into my very bones. I press my eyes shut tightly. The servants pass by us without a word. Their attention fixated on us for as long as they can before they've passed us and it'd be too rude for them to turn and gawk.

Yes, this is it. I needed this. I needed *touch*. I needed to feel close to someone and not just a guest in a foreign home.

Kai waits until I step back. He has a different sort of glow when we pull away. Perhaps we're more alike than I'd thought. Perhaps... Kai needs physical affection too.

"Thank you." I give him a small curtsey, pulling at the scraps of my skirt.

"Thank you." Kai fiddles with the buttons of his white shirt. "It's, uh, been a long time since someone has given me a genuine hug."

Oh. I think back to the handcuffs. Kai doesn't have *lovers* he has *fuck buddies*.

"That's very sad." I crinkle my nose. "Well I'm around if you need another one."

"I'll keep that in mind."

His yellow eyes stay on me as I step into my room. I give him a slight wave, closing the door.

"I'll be packed and ready for tomorrow." I remind

him just before I close it all the way. I wait, against the door, until I hear his footsteps fade down the hallway.

Anticipation, excitement, fear, anxiety, adrenaline, I'm not sure what emotion consumes me like fire. My veins are hot with it.

Carefully, I undo the thin straps on my heels and let them fall to the floor. My bare feet slap against the black and white tile. I dodge the furniture. A fire has been lit in the hearth for the evening, its heat waves over me as I jog by.

I don't have a bag to pack with. At least not a duffle bag or even old grocery bags like what I had wadded up for days under my sink in the apartment. As soon as I open the closet door, light cascades down over the assortment of clothing that's filled it. Gowns, gowns, and more gowns. Ranging from scandalous, to porn inspired.

Whatever this "long hard trip" is, gowns will not do. I can't do anything in these slips of material. Not unless we are paying this seer with a brief flash of my chest. *To be clear, we are NOT paying the seer with a glimpse of my prize winning ta-tas.*

There is a wall of shoes, very few without heels. Slowly, I pan through them and find my old worn boots hidden amongst them. I grab them and hug the worn leather to me, the soles still smelling of my feet as I squeeze. *Ah, my long-lost boots!* What a reuniting moment. These have to come with. My boots have gotten me through more hard times than anything else.

Well, with the exception of Jase. The thought crosses my mind, fleeting and sorrowful.

Beside the shoes I find hooks. Purses. Mainly small clutches covered in rhinestones. Though, as I hoped, there's a small option of oversized purses—totes. The largest bags hanging from the highest hooks, as if to discourage me from using them. I stretch on my toes, my fingers not even close enough to brush their fine materials.

Pouting, I look around for anything to reach up and knock it from its home. Nothing. So, as a last resort, I begin scaling the shelves for the shoes. Slowly at first, to get a feel for how sturdy the structure of it is. Under foot, the wood holds without a bend or protesting groan. A sure sign I'm safe to proceed.

My fingers clasp each shelf, holding on only with the whisper of the prayer on my lips. Sweat builds in my grip, under my fingers, making my hands slide ever so gently. I stretch a few shelves up, grazing along the edge of the bag. It swings on its hook.

I let out a huff of hair and clamber one shelf higher. This time I grab a shoe off its shelf and swing for the bag. My momentum plucks it from the hanger, just as it plucks me from my perch.

A nervous scream, unbecoming of a queen, leaves me. Wood scratches against my calves, my hands finally slipping from the shelves. I land roughly on my heels, teetering backward only to stumble to my butt. The ringing of my head hitting the metal hanger rod on the way down repeats, as pain blossoms in my skull.

I lay at the bottom of my closet with my eyes pressed tightly closed. *A queen would have asked a servant to get it down for them. You don't have to climb your closet, Briar.* I scold myself.

A knot is already forming, sore to the touch, at the top of my crown. My shins feel rough, white and red scratches trail up them. Even my ankles, that took the brunt of my fall, ache.

So not the best start to whatever hard and long travel I'd be doing tomorrow...but it seems like just my luck.

Standing, I test my ankles. They hold me up even if they hurt. Every heartbeat in my head throbs in pain. Hopefully, I'll sleep it off. Still, in victory the bag has fallen to the floor!

I smile. *Maybe it's just that I'm an independent person and I don't need a servant to fetch my things.*

The zipper opens easily to reveal the deep purse, enough to hold a few days' worth of clothing. With little hope, I scan the closet for clothes. I'm NOT travelling in dresses. I refuse.

Wobbling slightly on each step, I move to a dresser. The drawers glide open, many filled with straight lingerie for sleeping. I can't travel in that. Nope, not that either. When Kai said I should pack, what exactly did that mean to him?

The last drawer, I pull open with low expectations, is stuffed so full it hardly opens. I yank as I catch the blue of denim. Jeans. Oh, my god there are jeans. One last yank, and the drawer pops open.

It's more than jeans. It's sweatpants, joggers, leggings, different colored denims. And t-shirts! *Is this from my mortal closet?* I squeal, unable to contain my excitement. I understand holding to this fucking ruse in the Iron Court but I don't think I've ever been more filled with joy by regular everyday clothes in my entire life.

I wish I was one of those girls who relished being in finery, but all I ever find myself thinking is how exposed or uncomfortable I am. Jeans and a t-shirt for life, baby. Leafing through the items, even going as far as to bring the materials to my face to breathe in the old scent of my apartment. I pick a few shirts and multiple jeans.

A shade of sorrow constricts my heart. It all smells so... homey. Like a long-ago cherished memory. I stuff the items into the bag.

Slowly, I settle myself onto my knees. My vision blurs, losing focus on my surroundings. The taste of home makes me only hungrier for normalcy.

Lincoln? I test the boundaries between us. His wall exists as it has, in the annoying way he put it up. I imagine walking up to it, knocking politely. *Lincoln, I know you're there.*

Does he deserve my politeness when he left me with so little before I came here? You know what? No. I bang on the wall of his mind. I deserve his attention and a fucking explanation. Biting my lip, I force myself to push down the thoughts of how quickly I return to him, how quickly my mind finds a home in him. It's probably just this unasked-for bond. But don't think about it.

Lincoln Ziko. I scream. The tension traveling through my body as I clench my fists.

With a blink, his wall falls. Lincoln strolls into my mind with a nonchalance and unprecedented confidence.

Briar Anders. There is a smile on Lincoln's lips, a warmth I can sense that makes me mimic the movement. *Has my family overwhelmed you yet?*

Understatement of the fucking year. I scrub at my face as if that could wash away all my feelings of unease.

You're hurt? My head echoes with his urgency. *What happened?*

I'm not... I'm fine. I just fell trying to get something out of the closet. Why didn't you warn me the closet was going to be bigger than my old apartment?

What did you expect from a castle? A cupboard with clothes stuffed in it?

Lincoln, it's its own room! I chuckle. Zipping the bag, I toss it to the floor and kick at the dresser to close the drawer.

Did you... do you need something? Lincoln asks.

What do I say? I miss you. I miss our friendship... our whatever the fuck it is. I'm mad at you? I'm frustrated that you left me with an unsatisfying goodbye?

I'm sorry. About the good-bye, I mean. He responds. Right, because he's in my thoughts. *I'm not very good at those. And Briar... you're something.*

Something?

You're tempting. In all the ways you shouldn't be. All the ways that make me weak. I can't express to you the extent to which we could never be and how much I also wish we could. I miss you. I miss our friendship, too.

My hand covers my lips, as if I could hide myself and the goofy grin from him. I let the closet door close behind me, and pull the bed covers up to slip under.

If I'm queen I can change things.

Not to that degree. You'll see. You'll still be held to the standards of your counsel.

Then I'll rid myself of the counsel.

It doesn't work like that.

I sigh, pulling the blankets up to my chin. *I don't, uh, I don't want to think about that right now. I just want to feel normal. And seeing as this is kind of, sort of, like texting but mentally I think it will help. Can we just talk about regular things?*

I've never texted a day in my life.

Just think of it like a metaphor. You know what... just don't worry about it. What are you doing?

Like right now? His thoughts shift with unease.

Yes.

I'm laying in bed.

Warmth cocoons around me, but I stretch out a hand on the sheets and imagine Lincoln propped against the pillows. *Me too,* I answer softly.

Between blinks, Lincoln's image sprawled out in loose fitting black pants, always without a shirt, appears on my bed. I gasp. My fingers go through his hand, reaching for mine, as if he is a ghost.

I'm projecting. I'm still in your head, a figment of your imagination, if you will. No one else can see me.

You should be like this all the time. My skin tingles as I hover my hand over his.

It's rather tiresome, but seeing as I'm about the go to sleep, I'd say it's worth the energy.

His long dark hair falls to the side of his forehead as he leans to his side. His gaze, the iron cut pupil I'd missed seeing, fans over me. My fingers long to touch the hair on his chest, my lips wishful for a kiss. He's just a figment of my imagination... untouchable.

"I miss you," I say out loud.

He nods. *I miss your annoyingly mortal self as well. Are you getting along with my brothers? Rowan is quite the hands-on type of man.*

"Oh, he's already confessed that he is pursuing me." I try not to smirk. "But Kai... Kai has surprised me."

Oh?

"He's... kind, and funny. He gives me my space but also knows when to not."

He's a prince and he's been trained well.

"I met your mother. And she is truly awful. Rowan says your father is a god? Is that true?"

Well, I haven't met him so I couldn't tell you. His shoulders shake with a small chuckle. *And my mother is a special breed. Like most of the Fae you'll be facing in your council or in other Courts.*

"I wish I could touch you." I draw a line down his abdomen, his image flickering as I do.

You just love to break the rules.

"What can I say? I'm a rebel." I pause. "Would you let me touch you again? Despite the way you're convinced we could never be?"

Why? Do you have more pent up energy that needs to be released? I'm sure Rowan would do the trick if you need a quick fuck.

I don't hide the way I scowl or roll my eyes. "Lincoln, I'm not fucking your brother. *I* don't understand how *you* don't understand how totally messed up that is. I want to touch you. I want to fight for you. I have my mind set on you." I give him a sly smile. "And I can be pretty stubborn when I set my mind to something."

And you've set your mind on me?

"Yes. I want you to fight for us. I'll fight for you, too."

That's a slippery slope.

"Let's slide down it together."

I'm not sure you know what you're asking.

"I don't care."

Ha, of course you don't. His image dissolves, his mental barrier slamming back up.

"Lincoln?" My hand bounces off the bed.

I have to go.

Then he's gone. Like he is always gone. It leaves me only to wonder if I finally said the wrong thing? Perhaps taking a page out of Rowan's book just doesn't work in this situation. Did I just fuck up?

THE GANUSH MOUNTAINS

Two knocks at my door is all I'm granted, though I expected much less. I've picked nearly three eye-boogers from the crevasses of my tear ducts, but somehow sleep still clings to my eyelashes. The force of Rowan letting himself into my bedchambers creates a breeze that doesn't touch my bare skin.

With many thanks to whoever gave me the smallest sliver of my mundane life back, I've donned a dark washed pair of jeans, my boots, and an oversized t-shirt that I thrifted. The dagger Kai had gifted me for the time being sticks awkwardly out of the waistband of my jeans. Collin would have hated this outfit; I think with a smile. Lincoln would have loved it enough to take it right off... in the best of ways. I smirk.

"No lingerie today?" Rowan teeters in with less layers than I've ever seen him wear.

"I could say the same for you. Where are your coats

upon coats upon coats?" I point out, pulling my bag onto my shoulder.

"What can I say? I like to travel light." He winks.

Kai's long hair has been braided down his scalp, wearing a similar pant and loose-fitting shirt to his brother. Both in colors of black and grey. "I think I like you better dressed like this." The prince gives me a once over.

"More fitting, don't you think?"

"Yes," he purrs. "Rowan, take her bag. And Briar," He pulls his bag off his shoulders and tugs a long brown belt from it. "This will help you carry that dagger much more comfortably. Also will protect it from getting dinged up."

Stiff with annoyance, Rowan pulls my bag off my shoulder. Thin leather straps hold a backpack to his wide frame. He shrugs the bag off to reveal metal buckles that he attaches my purse to.

"Thank you, you didn't have to." I wave it off to both brothers, taking the belt from Kai and securing it and the dagger to my waist.

"Actually, I did." Rowan sends his brother an unamused look.

Kai smiles and offers his arm. He smells of warmed honey and charcoal. I try not to obviously breathe it in as I loop my arm through his and let him lead me out of the room. I'd awoken eager and early enough to be patiently waiting near my door for the last thirty minutes. The necklace, my powers, rests heavily on my neck.

"Well, the portal will get us near enough. But the seer lives in the Ganush Mountain range."

"So you're telling me that I'm going to have to climb a mountain today?" Maybe I didn't dress well enough...

"Rowan and I will both be there to help. It's totally okay."

Is it though?

"Plus what we are climbing isn't exactly a mountain..." Rowan adjusts the bag on his back.

The curtains on the balcony have already been opened, the days warmth travelling down the halls. With the sun behind us our shadows stretch over the floor. Kai watches me even as I watch the ground.

"Is that *the* necklace?" He points.

"Uh, yeah." I glance at Rowan, gingerly touching my neck.

"Don't worry. He's up to speed."

"Should I be offended that you didn't trust me enough to tell me, love?" Rowan trudges up beside me.

If anyone should be offended, it's probably me. Kai didn't really have a right to share my personal information with Rowan.

"Why is he coming again?" I say with heavy sarcasm. Rowan laughs, bumping me playfully with his shoulders.

"Two pairs of hands protecting our Mortal Queen are better than one," Kai suggests.

"This is why I need this done." I shrug. "I don't want anyone to *have* to do the protecting."

"Oh, you're never going to escape that." Rowan

reminds me. "You're a queen. You're royalty. Someone is always going to be trying to protect you. While someone else is also always trying to kill you."

Damn.

The three of us, all incredibly casually dressed, turn toward the front doors of the long hallway that runs the length of the castle. I run through Rowan's quick tour of the castle trying to distinguish where the portals might be. He didn't mention any that I know of.

"Where are your portals? Do you not have a hallway filled with them like the Shadow Court?"

"No. Oh, most certainly not. Mother frowns upon such heavy traveling. She says it only creates more Shadow Fae." Kai tilts his head from side to side contemplating the idea. "She isn't totally wrong." He offers a smile.

"Our portals are mostly spread amongst the forest, the one we walked to on your first visit here. You fell right into my arms that day. Do you remember that?" Rowan nudges me with his elbow again.

"Yes, I do."

"Well, she's certainly fallen back out of your arms since then." Kai reaches for the large iron doors. He does nothing more than wave his hand before they swing wide. "We talked about this. You've got to back off."

"I'm not touching her." He scoffs. "I told you I wasn't going to touch her." Rowan points his long lashes at me, batting them. "Unless she asks."

"I probably won't be doing that anytime soon." I suggest, as casually as I can.

"A shame."

"Ignore him," Kai adjusts his own backpack. "He wasn't raised to have the manners it takes to be heir."

Kai's jab feels more like the cutting slash of a blade. Rowan walks through the doors, letting them close loudly behind us without even showing his offense. Though, the tips of his ears, poking out of his braids do turn a brilliant red.

This is going to be a long trip.

"So," I clear my throat. I watch my steps carefully, as I maneuver the couple of steps down to the stone path that leads to the woods. My ankles still mildly hold the pain of my fall from grace last night. "How do I make sure I don't randomly go through a portal?"

"Well they're clearly marked." Kai says, reluctantly adding. "For Fae eyes."

"Little Mortal eyes may have trouble making out the markings between the trees. So just step where we step and—Briar! What did you do to your head?" Rowan stops behind me. He reaches for the goose egg, from the night before that's appeared since my head met the innerworkings of my closet in such a personal way, stopping himself before his hand touches it.

My hand trails up into my hair, rubbing it gently. The knot is still tender to every brush of my fingers.

"Is it that bad? That big?" I breathe. Maybe I should have looked in the mirror better if it's that noticeable.

"You have a second head growing on your head." Rowan lifts his chin, examining it.

"Stop looking at it. I'm fine." I step away.

Two warm hands clasp my arms, holding me in my spot. Kai's eyebrows turn to one as he scrunches them together. "You're bruised. Who did this to you?"

I slither out from his hands, swatting him away as he tries to reach for me again. A blush creeps up my neck. And now I have to tell them that I did it to myself?

"Just forget about it. We have places to go." I take a step. In the same heartbeat both Kai and Rowan dart from behind me to form a new wall in front of me. I cross my arms over my chest. "Seriously?"

"Seriously," Kai deadpans.

"Fine. Fine. No one did anything to me. I did it to me. I went to pack my bag last night like you asked but the only real option was that large freaking *purse*. Is it too much to ask for you Fae to own duffle bags?"

"What's a duffle bag?" Rowan frowns.

"It's like a peasant's suitcase," Kai whispers back, waving me on to continue.

"Anyway, I couldn't reach the bag so I climbed the shoe rack."

Rowan covers his mouth with his hand to hide a smile. "You climbed it?"

"Yeah, I climbed it. Then I promptly fell off of it and banged my head when I fell backwards onto my butt." We'll just purposefully leave out the part where I may have also sprained both my ankles.

The Princes look to one another and I prepare myself for some sort of lecture. When they turn back to face me, they fall against one another, bending to hold themselves at their knees as they sputter with laughter.

"Cupcake," Kai holds the bridge of his nose. "You could have used a servant for help. Or asked me this morning." He turns to his brother. "We may have more work cut out for us than anticipated on this trip."

"Stop!" I step off the path around the brothers. "It was an accident. I'm not usually that clumsy." Then, as if on cue—the entire punchline of the joke—my foot slips on the lip of the trail as I try to step back on it and my feet stumble over themselves.

Broad hands wrap around my shoulders, pulling me upright. Kai does nothing to hide his knowing smirk.

"Children learn to walk, only if they first learn how to fall."

His proverb is probably well meaning. Probably. But right now, it's annoying as fuck.

"I was going to catch myself." I push his hands off me.

"What? With your face?" Rowan snorts pushing past us both. "I'll lead."

With my face. Is it childish of me to mock him right now? Yes. Regrettably, and most stupidly, yes.

"Come now, my sweet." Kai guides me forward. "Off to find you some magic so you can walk like the rest of the grownups."

"Okay, now you're just making fun of me."

"Was I not making fun of you before?"

I trail an eye over the prince. "I'm not sure I'm enjoying this banter."

"Only because you're the brunt of the joke, human." Rowan calls over his shoulder as the shadow of the trees falls over him.

Dew still shines on the leaves. Vines weave up the old bark and onto the branches that hide us from the sky. Animals don't call like they do in the evening, most probably still hiding in their holes not ready to wake for the day. I don't blame them. If it wasn't for the excitement of something new, of an answer to the question I've been asking for some time now, I would still be hiding under the covers until one of the Ziko siblings rolled into my room and demanded something of me.

The stone of the trail is replaced with brush and broken twigs. I'm more careful of my steps now that there is so much more to trip on. If I embarrass myself in front of these men one more time then I'll just go ahead and dig myself a grave. No thank you.

"So how long is this trip?" I ask, trying to pass the time and fill the silence.

"As long as it takes a human to climb a mountain, if I'd have to guess." Kai squints trying to look through the branches. I follow his gaze, wondering what he could be looking for. My eyesight proves to be less helpful.

"Do you have any experience with rock climbing?" Rowan sends me a look over his shoulder. His braids make a gentle noise as they smack against his leather backpack.

"Rowan, I grew up in fucking New York City. Do you think I have rock climbing experience?"

"I'm not entirely sure what the city you grew up in has much to do with it. But judging by your lack of overall balance, I'd have to guess probably not."

"No, I don't." I admit. Also, I'm out of shape, I think but don't add. "There aren't many places to go climb mountains in the city and even if there was I've never had that sort of money to just go out and do it on a whim."

"On a whim." Kai echoes. "I have lots of whims."

Oh, I bet you do.

"Yes, you're a prince. You have enough money to have whims. Regular people do not."

"So you were a peasant before?" Rowan says, he crinkles his nose, offended at his own statement and the fact that I'm broker than broke.

"I was not a fucking peasant. Don't call people that. Or Fae for that matter. God, how rude."

"Like you said, we're princes... we can call people whatever we please. Comes with the title." He sticks out his tongue. "That means you soon can too."

"I'd rather not." I place my palm against the nearest tree, the bark rough against my skin. It balances me as I step over a small broken tree limb and an overgrown bush. Kai's hands hover near my waist waiting to catch me if need be. "I'm not going to fall." I reassure him.

"Promise?" Kai whispers, his face near enough I'm certain the word could only be caught by the two of us.

"Promise," I say slowly.

"Almost there!" Rowan calls as he grows farther ahead. The space between us continues to multiply and I have to wonder if he is using some Fae superpower to get ahead or if he truly walks that fast.

I huff. Rowan catches the noise and turns on the toe of his boots, breaking a twig in half under foot. "Too fast for you human? It's going to take us a whole damn week to get up this mountain if this is the pace you're going to go."

"Who even asked you to come? I know I didn't."

Kai hums with laughter behind me. At least he's enjoying this. Sweat has already built along my brows and the day isn't even particularly warm. Maybe I've just been too lazy. Maybe I should start going for runs.

But I don't see these Fae sprinting around the castle. It's got to be the magic. How is it going to change me? Will it hurt when it's released? Will it feel good? The naughty part of me has to guess what the odds on it happening to give me some sort of an orgasm. They've hinted at sex helping me be able to release my powers. God, I hope I don't have to have sex with someone to get it. At least not either of these two men hanging out with me now.

"Can you see the carvings in these two trees?" Kai asks. He lifts a hand, pointing over my shoulder, to the trees that Rowan's posed himself in front of.

Between the long trunks nothing appears to be all that different. I expect the black void I'm used to falling into but all I see is the wind rustle some blooms of honeysuckle just yards behind it. Shouldn't it flicker or something? Or maybe look kind of fuzzy?

I try to focus on the trees, like Kai has suggested. Bark... bark... rougher looking tree bark. Green moss... some type of bug. No, no engravings, no markings, no sign or flashing lights that say 'Hello, you are now leaving the Iron Court, please enjoy your trip to the Ganush Mountain Range.'

"I see... two trees." I finally concede.

"Human eyes," Rowan tsks.

"Why is there no black void to fall into?"

"Oh, there is a void all right. Would you like me to hold you tight as we fall?" Rowan grins and steps toward me.

I shake my head, stepping back into Kai.

"Okay, so my brother isn't very good at backing off. And to amend his previous statement, the void in these types of portals is much smaller and more condensed. You don't *need* to hold onto anyone. You'll just step through and it will feel like you're falling for a moment but don't adjust your step because when it hits the ground you'll be on the other side."

"Why is it different?"

"Made with different intents," Kai suggests. "I'm not sure, really. These are gentler to go through though. Do you trust me?" He steps around me, heading for the trees. Before he reaches them, he offers his hand.

"See you on the other side." Rowan blows me a kiss before dissolving between the trees.

Do you trust me? That was the question Lincoln had asked me before I let him combine our minds. My answer then had been no. Not just no, but heck no. But do I regret letting him invade my thoughts? Not entirely. Though that could change if he ever marries and it isn't me. But I'm not going to think about that.

My answer now is much faster, more easily said. "Yes."

I place my hand in his. Kai's gaze moves from my face to our palms. When he looks back up, his eyes shine with something far too human. It's clear the Fae have a range of emotions but in my experience they're all just muted versions of our own. The glint in his gaze isn't just sadness... It's heartbreak. Nevertheless, he smiles, and blinks away anything remotely questionable.

My intrigue gets swallowed. Kai gives my hand the slightest squeeze pulling me forward as he backs between the trees.

"Remember, don't change your stride. The steps are just a little farther down than you expect. You can do this, Cupcake."

"If you keep calling me that I'm going to have to give you some sort of nickname that's related to a baked good. How do you like Brownie? Or Cookie?" I step forward, letting him guide me.

His head tilts back with a laugh and he steps through the portal. The sound I expect to come from him is suddenly gone. My shoulder protests as he gives a firm yank.

I step through the trees. It's black like the inside of my eyelids, or maybe it's just that I truly am blinking. I imagine a step, then my boot moves through the air of the expected bottom. The top half of my body leans forward and I'm sure I'll tumble or that the other side has never even existed at all.

When I'm certain that my toes will never meet solid ground, my boot scuffs through dirt. I look down. Tall, wet green grass is bent at an odd angle around my boots, Kai's hand is still holding mine. But behind him, behind Rowan, and behind the continuous expanse of tropical forest, an ash mountain rises.

Then another.

And another.

The Ganush mountain range.

WISHING SPIRIT

"You survived." Rowan claps me on my back.

Kai drops my hand, looking up to the steep high terrain we'll be walking through shortly. Humidity suffocates the air. Even the hair in my peripheral vision starts to frizz and quickly grows in size. I'd imagine my hair will be as big as the mountain by the time night falls.

The mountains of Ganush, the word even sounds funny when I'm merely thinking it, aren't what I expect from a mountain. When I pictured them before it was tall peaks, capped in snow. I even have a jacket messily shoved into the purse attached to Rowan's bag. (Who folds their clothes now-a-days?) There doesn't appear to be any splash of white snow on any of these mountain peaks.

"I didn't know it was going to be so hot," I confess.

"Warm and humid. I could have probably warned you. A prepared traveler is one that does not go blindly to his death." Kai bobs his head, reaching into his pocket and pulling out a black elastic. "Here, for your hair."

"Gah, your old proverbs are going to scare her. We are not walking into certain death." Rowan assures me. "I mean... most likely we aren't." Then he adds a wink.

I offer them both some version of a pathetic laugh as I stand and tie up my hair. My skin is already sticky. We haven't even really begun our journey and I'm sweating in places I wish I was not. Hopefully, these jeans don't betray me and show the puddle of sweat that's making my underwear damp. Now that would be embarrassing. I can hear the boys joking about it now.

"Thank you." I point to the hair tie. "I'm surprised you had one on hand."

"Well, I know how bothersome loose hair can be, especially in a climate like this." He gestures to his own braided hair.

"I should have known. It's just not that common where I'm from for men to have long hair. Still, I appreciate you sharing."

It really is very sad that more human men don't wear their hair long. It's quite handsome. I mean, I'm looking at Exhibit A and B right now.

Kai smiles gently before looking up. Rowan joins him in peering onward. As far as I can see with my mortal gaze, there are no easily identifiable paths. Trees and the occasional rock formation jut off at odd angles. It's hard to see it all through the canopy above us.

"Think it best to start this way?" Kai points.

"Yes, though I imagine Briar will need a boost to make it up. Surely, it's doable." Rowan sniffs the air. "Do you smell that?"

Neither brother is looking at me as I wait patiently behind them. Casually, I try to sniff the air too. It smells like dirt and wet grass. Actually, it's somewhat calming in a way. I take another breath. It smells like sweet blooms or maybe lavender. I note that there aren't any flower beds within eyesight.

"Yes," Kai spins slowly in a circle, his attention skipping over me as he watches the forest around us. "It's likely lurking nearby. Hopefully it hasn't spotted us yet, but it'll be on our scent soon enough. We better get moving."

"It?" I clear my throat.

"Come now." Rowan waves and starts forward. Kai lingers, letting me walk in front of him.

"Okay, but I'm going to need a little bit of an explanation or else I'll start to worry."

"Girls worrying is quite annoying," Rowan mutters.

"Shut up," I snap, then look over my shoulder much more pleasantly to Kai. "Is it another panther? Or some sort of feline thing that's much larger than it should be?"

"No. It's something not entirely real."

Even here at the base of the mountain the ground has begun to slope more and more. I can only imagine what sort of workout my calves will be having. It's dreadful to even think about. More so now that there is a not so real something-or-other that's about to be on our scent. Sounds just as deadly as the stupid metaphor Kai shared.

"Explain," I deadpan.

"It's a Wishing Spirit. Some say it's what we Fae turn into when we die with regret or unfinished business. Dreadful things." Kai keeps his tone even, but every so often he looks over his shoulder behind us. "They aren't physical. Not unless you touch them."

"What do they look like?"

"That's... up to you." Rowan smiles. "If a second version of me appears I'll know you're secretly in love with me."

"Not likely."

"You'll see the spirit as whatever you are wishing for, whatever your soul needs," Kai says.

"What exactly were you smelling?"

Small sprouts of trees grow up around us. I grab onto one, using it as leverage to help me forward. Ahead of us, the trees wither away to burnt stumps and skinny new blooming twigs bursting out of black rock. I blatantly sniff the air.

"I don't smell anything."

"Well not only will you see the spirit as what you want, it sort of takes over all of your senses. It'll smell like your heart's desire too. If you touch it, it will take a physical form and *feel* real. Deceptive in every way." Kai lags behind me by a few feet.

"So what did you both smell?"

"That's personal." Rowan looks back at me. "Do you think we are going to tell you what we desire the most? No. First thing they tell you in prince training is *not* to share your most valuable secrets."

"What do you think I'm going to do with this information? Sell it to the highest bidder?"

"Well you are going to be a queen that rules in a different court, Briar," Kai suggests.

"Watch out, that almost felt like a threat," I laugh at him.

Kai gives me a smug smile. "Can't be too careful."

"When I get these powers unlocked," I suggest as if it's a new level in a video game, "I'll be able to kick your butt for saying such offensive, untrusting things."

"I'd like to see you try," Rowan chuckles.

"Don't get ahead of yourself." Kai waves me off, as I turn and walk backwards so I can see him. I pause, letting him get closer.

"I'll give you that good old one, two, jab." I punch at the air. Kai dodges easily.

"You think you're smooth. You best--" He stops talking, his body pausing as he perks up like a hound dog.

"Damn that was fast," Rowan snarls. "What's the plan, brother?"

"What? Is it the Wishing Spirit?" Automatically, I start looking around.

"Don't look around!" Kai barks. He turns me around. "Keep going. The options are not to make contact with it, let it stay in its spirit form and harass us for as long as it pleases or one of us can touch it and we can go for the kill."

Rowan drags a hand down his pale features. "Making it physical could mean using a lot of energy to fight it. Not to mention protecting the obviously weak princess we have with us."

"Don't you mean queen," I interject. They both ignore me.

"Ignore the spirit it is, then." Kai tucks his fingers into the straps of his backpack and stares straight ahead. "It's getting closer. Briar, keep your gaze on the ground. No matter what you think you see, or hear, or smell, or whatever sort of sense it tries to appeal you with. And for the love of all, things holy, don't touch it."

"What could be so hard about that?" *I'll just channel my inner 'Collin'. He was great at ignoring me and he's an idiot so surely if he can do it so can I.*

"You'd be surprised."

On the next breeze the strong scent of lavender carries toward me again. My shoulders fall away from my ears. I take a deep breath thinking of the blooms that could produce such a lovely aroma. As soon as I relax, all my muscles tense again. Lavender... the flowers.... that's what I'd smelled earlier. I won't be allowing this Wishing Spirit to come in here and bribe me with a bouquet.

What an odd thing for me to smell. What do I desire so much that smells like wild flowers? Romance? Nah, that's fleeting. I try to concentrate on my thoughts to recognize on my own what I could potentially be up against with this spirit, but Kai's voice rips through my thoughts.

"It's here."

Then the spirit starts to talk. "Briar!" A woman's voice. "Briar! I can't believe that you found me."

I point my gaze to my shoes and reach for another flimsy sapling of a tree to pull myself up the volcano. The voice is inviting. The voice is... familiar. I repeat her phrases in my mind trying to place it.

"I can't believe it's you. It's really you," the voice says again.

From the edge of my vision a figure appears. Skirts catch on the rubble of the forest floor, but the girl, she moves closer, reaching for me. I dodge her hand with a gasp.

"You didn't tell me it was going to try and touch *me*..." I trail off as I look back at my own honey brown hair and dark blue eyes. The last I'd seen of her, her stomach was round and pregnant, now it's flat, and her face is youthful as I remember. She's younger than me. She died younger than me. Queen Amelia.

"Mom?" I whisper.

"I can't believe you would even recognize me. Honey, you've grown up to be so beautiful. Come now, come with me. I've got so much to tell you and it's dangerous for your two companions to know that I've lived. We need to go hide." Her eyes are kind, and she smiles at me like I'm the Christmas gift she's waited her whole entire life for... like I'm her missing child.

"It's not real," Kai whispers into my ear, pushing me forward. "I know you want it to be real. I do too. But it's not what you think it is. The spirit isn't your mother."

"Don't you dare say that to her!" The ghost of my mother pales. "I've waited my whole life to see my baby, to hold *my daughter* in my arms. You won't play me off as some figment of her imagination. You can see me can't you?" She points to Kai.

The Prince's attention is zeroed in on my back. His hand against my spine is the only thing that moves me forward. Ahead of us, Rowan groans and swats a fly away from his face.

"Do you see her?" I press, looking back at my mother. She looks so real, my heart aches knowing she's not.

"No," Kai says sternly. "I see me."

I know she's just a spirit projecting my need to be loved, my need to have a family, my every want to be a part of something... but if I could just look at her a little longer. All of me wants to memorize her face, make her less of the reflection of my own father's memory. I want her to be more than the painting that hangs in Queen Cordelia's room.

"You see yourself? That seems a little vain, don't you think?" I say, softly.

"Briar, my dear, don't listen to him. He sees me. They

aren't safe for you. It's safe with me. Come with me. Please." The spirit begs.

I squeeze my eyes shut and turn away. "Kai, I need you to talk to me right now."

"I see me," he repeats, his voice hoarse. "Me, crowned. Me, without my looming parents, without the restrictions they've placed on me."

"I didn't think we were sharing what we saw." Rowan pauses looking up at the suddenly steep climb over a large boulder. He bends ever so slightly at his knees before pouncing to land in a crouch above the rock.

I try to stare ahead at Rowan, not to give the false imagery of the mother I never had another glance, but she steps toward me. My foot catches along the root of a tree and Kai's arm shoots out behind me. He means well but the force of his hand hitting my back propels me back forward. I stumble again reaching to catch myself on anything I can grab.

My fingers hit flesh. Soft, with the slightest hint of a pinkish glow, I stare down at my grasp that encompasses a slender forearm. Blood drains from my face as Kai hisses through his clenched teeth. I look up. My mother smiles at me, gently.

Lavender fills my lungs. The urge to let her wrap her arms around me, to sob into her tattered dress, makes tension build in every muscle. She's real.

"M--", I open my mouth and her smile turns wicked. The gentle edges of her human teeth lengthen to points and black oozes from her mouth like thick saliva.

My hand slips from her soft skin, still tingling with the need for her touch. *It's not her. It never was her. I knew it all along and still a part of me wanted to believe it.* I curse myself as my feet pedal backward.

My mother's image is no longer in view. A single blonde braid flashes before me as Kai slips between us. His boot connects with the Wishing Spirit that lets out an undeniably inhuman scream. Any desire for what I thought was my mother is quickly replaced with a new fear.

Slipping against wet leaves, I scurry toward Rowan. I can't chance another glance back. I don't want the image of the Wishing Spirit turned devil in my mind's eye for a second longer.

"Rowan take her hand!" Kai shouts.

I'm stretching on my toes for Rowan's touch that extends along the rough stone's edge. My shirt rises and my midriff scraps along the pointed peaks. I try to use them as leverage to climb up to him. My boot slips from the small lips with every try.

"You're going to have to do better than that, human. Come on!" Rowan shouts, but his attention is split between me and everything I'm not willing to watch behind me.

There is a scuffle of movement behind me. I know it's some sort of fight that's raging between the Fae and the Spirit. And it's all from my touch. Kai bellows a scream, one laced with pain. It's followed by a crash and a repeat of the Spirit's wailing cry.

I gasp as I feel hands take my waist. "It's me," Kai groans and pushes me up toward his brother.

Rowan's hand curls around my forearm, he doesn't even sweat as he lifts me one handed onto the rock. I lay flat on my back, reeling. I flinch at every strike.

"You okay?" Rowan whispers.

"Me? Am I okay?" Only then do I roll to my stomach and watch Kai sling a sword through the air. Black blood splits out with a violent trajectory, the spirit's... my mother's... arm falling to the ground. I close my eyes. "Should you be asking if your brother is okay?"

"Oh, he's fine," he laughs. "This is nothing."

"It doesn't feel like nothing."

"Open your eyes, he's almost got it finished," Rowan encourages. He leans lower from his crouch, his lips brushing my ear. "As a queen you're probably going to have to witness a lot of worse things than Kai fighting a spirit. Hell, Cordelia herself can get pretty nasty and she's the one thing standing in your way."

"Can you... can you still see the spirit as it was? Does it still appear as whatever you were seeing it as?"

"No." He shakes his head, sending his small braids scattering across his leather backpack. "She looks like Queen Amelia. She looks like your mother. Is that why you don't want to look?"

"Are you asking me if I want to watch Kai kill what appears to be my mother?" I crack one eye at Rowan. He's still watching Kai. "The answer to that would be fuck no."

"I mean, I guess I get it. Also, I'm a tad disappointed

that you didn't see me. It would be pretty badass to watch me and my brother dueling right now. Even if I would have to be rooting for my brother's win."

"You could watch yourself die?" I finally sit up. I keep my back to Kai, though I can still hear his breath mingling with the Spirit's in their efforts.

"Eh," Rowan shrugs. "It's almost over—"

There's a gurgling sound, like water bubbling out of a child's cup. The noise softens. I jump as Kai pounces to standing on the rock next to me. Looking from his boots up to him, he looks grim as he pushes his sword back into his belt.

Carefully, I turn to look down into the forest. Black is splattered against the brilliant hues of the plants. Everything is tinted with blood. My mother stares back at me, her body lifeless. Against my lips, I feel my fingertips touching my mouth to hold in the tremble of a horrified sob. I hadn't even realized I'd moved.

Had she looked like this in her death? Was she just as beautiful as she remains now as when she was beheaded while the kingdom watched? Cordelia's mother took everything away from me. Cordelia took it away from me. My deepest desire isn't the love of a man, it isn't power of a fucking kingdom, my deepest desire is a fucking parents love.

"It bit you," Rowan stands.

Kai holds out his arm, examining the bite. He offers his unharmed side and I take his hand and rise. Teeth marks, the perfect crescent of a human bite, breaks through his flesh. Black mingles with the red of his blood. More than that, the veins extending from the bite are tinted black as if the spirit's bad energy is seeping into his being.

"Oh my god." I grab his wrist and pull it toward me.

"Uh, ow." Kai blinks.

"Are you going to be okay?"

Slouching, I look at the bite even closer, praying that he hasn't been injected with venom or something else just as hideous. Kai shakes off my hands.

"It's fine."

"Did she poison you? Don't you lie to me Kai Ziko!" I shake a finger at him.

"Cupcake," he flashes me a brilliant grin, "If you think I'm going to let an annoying Wishing Spirit take me out of this world then you are sorely mistaken."

"Well, Buttercup," I try the nickname, "Sue me for being worried."

"Sue you?" Rowan tosses the Wishing Spirit one last look, frowning at the mess that surrounds it.

Kai brushes his sleeve down to cover the bite and adjust the backpack on his shoulders. They turn toward the mountain again.

"We better get moving. There are more of those, I'm sure." Kai moves into the new tree lined incline.

"I'm still confused what 'suing you' means. Does it have anything to do with being sexual?"

"I'm not sure how many times it has to be repeated but, like, not everything is sexual, Rowan."

"That's debatable." He points at me, grinning.

"No," I shake my head and do my best to keep up behind them. Walking away, I fight the need to give my mother's body one last look. "Suing someone...," I explain to keep my mind from dwelling, "is when they do something harmful to you or break the law or... something like that," Maybe I'm not good at explaining this. "Anyway, you take them to court and you get money out of them for whatever the reason is."

Sure, yeah, that explains it.

Rowan's eyes narrow. "What?"

"It's not like our Court. It's their law system. It's run by multiple people in her area instead of just the rule of their King or Queen," Kai tries to explain.

"Why would I want money from you?"

"How do you know so much but visit the human world so little?" I raise an eyebrow at the golden-haired prince.

"I once had relations with a lawyer of sorts," Kai doesn't bother to look back at us as he forges a path forward.

"Seriously, I'm confused," Rowan tries again.

"You know what... just forget it." I sigh.

A silence falls between us. As quiet as the sound of our feet hitting the mountainside and the angry huff of my breath can be. Every noise reminds me of the high-pitched screaming of the Wishing Spirit. Every blink, I see my mother's face.

I wonder if in her death she was content. I wonder if saving me was all she really needed.

I wonder if I would have made her proud.

I wonder if I'm making her proud now as I cling to every jutting tree and follow behind the princes of the Iron Court.

TEN

CAVERN CAMPING

Everything in my body begs for rest. My eyes drop and I know I must look like Kai when he is high. I keep my attention focused on his back. Rowan trails behind me.

"Quit staring at my ass," I breathe.

"It's a nice ass." Rowan replies.

Through Kai's sleeve I can see where black is seeping into the grey fabric as it clings to his arm. His energy since the encounter hasn't dwindled. Maybe he's right, the bite isn't an issue at all.

Though I realize Kai hasn't taken Reminints since we began the trip. The lack of Reminints may soon be a problem. Kai's arm pulls away from the branch he pushes down and breaks under his boot. His fingers tremble. The only sign his body isn't at peace.

A loud caw echoes over our heads as a bird takes flight. Its wingspan cuts across the clouds that ripple across the sky. The sun has moved down, hiding behind the mountain side. Only a little bit of light spills down to us. Occasionally, I take a look back down and our efforts have gotten us far enough up that the view is quite breathtaking. If I stop for even a moment though, I begin to lose Kai among the trees. And being behind along with Rowan sounds like a terrible idea at this point.

"I'm going to need a break," I say, ashamed of the limitations of my body.

"There's a small cave just up ahead. We'll make camp for the night. We should reach the seer by midday tomorrow. Though, I expect that she already knows we are here."

"Couldn't she make it easy and come to us? Meeting us mid-way would be the polite thing to do."

"If you want, I could carry you," Rowan offers.

"I'd rather walk till my feet bleed."

"Ooooo," He inhales through his teeth. "Why must you always play hard to get like that? You know I just want what's best for my queen."

"If you keep talking like that I'm going to throw up in my mouth." I turn back to him and roll my eyes. "And seriously, quit looking at my ass!"

"Some things just can't be helped, Briar."

"Well soon I'm not going to be able to help the foot that meets your balls."

Kai laughs. It's the most I've heard out of him since the Spirit.

Finally, the trees split enough that I'm able to see the cave's mouth up ahead. It's enough to motivate me to move faster. It's the last little bit I have to make and then I can rest. I didn't pack anything to sleep with...I remember. *Oops.* But I won't say anything out loud because then Rowan will just tell me that I can sleep with him. As if that does me any good.

Kai notices the increase in my pace and moves faster too, and much swifter. He slings the backpack from his shoulders and chucks it into the cave, pulling himself up onto the rock. This isn't too tall for me this time. I cling to the edge and my boots scamper up the side. Rolling ungracefully, I topple into the cave. Rowan's already inside when I sit up.

I melt back down onto the cave floor. Everything in this forest is just covered in its own sweat. Even the surface of the rock, cushioned by a thin layer of moss, makes my clothing damp with more than just my perspiration. I lift my arms over my head, trying to stretch myself out. Both men are pulling things out of their bags and when I think neither are looking, I take a big whiff of my underarm.

Ripe. Definitely not fresh. Lovely.

Then there is another smell. I'm certain isn't me. I turn away from my own body odor and sniff the breeze as it passes the mouth of the cave. Lavender.

I shoot upright, blood rushing painfully to my head. "I smell lavender."

"What?" Rowan says slowly. "All I smell is you."

"You better mean that in a very wonderful way," I snap at him even though I'm very aware of how utterly awful I reek myself. "No, I smell lavender. It's what I smelled when the Wishing Spirit was near."

Kai sniffs the air and Rowan follows suit.

"I don't smell anything." Rowan says again.

Kai moves past his brother, dropping his bag at his feet. He walks beyond me, extending himself as far as he can without teetering off the edge. I watch, unable to move.

His soft chuckle breaks the following silence.

At least this is laughable for him.

"There actually is a small lavender patch. It's a little out of sort for the area but I have a feeling it is some sort of spell. I'm sure the seer uses lavender every now and again."

I flatten myself back against the cave floor. Kai walks with loud steps as he goes back to his bag. Every movement he makes is deliberate and somehow there is a comfort in knowing that he wants me aware of where he is at all times. Rowan walks smoother, it's harder to pick up the sound of his movement.

"Water?" Rowan offers.

I open my eyes and find him sitting with his legs folded underneath him, not even a foot away. He holds out a small metal container. The humidity clings to my skin, I can even taste it in the back of my throat. But still, my body craves the water. I've probably sweated out half my body weight on the way up here.

With a thankful smile, I reach for the canister. As my fingers brush his he pulls it away.

"Ah, ah, ah," he teases, "I'll let you have a sip if you give me a kiss."

"Fuck off, Rowan!" I push myself further away.

He inches himself closer. "Just a little peck on the cheek. You've already kissed me once, what's the big deal?"

"I'm not using my body to make bargains with you." I give him my darkest stare and pray that it burns some sort of hole into his soul. Rowan is like that creepy friend you have that just never gets the hint. Take the damn hint, Rowan!

"What if--"

Rowan shoots upright, his toes scraping against the floor to find purchase. Kai's hands are wrapped in the fabric of his shirt pulling it away from Rowan's thick chest.

"I have had it! That's enough. If I knew that I was going to have to listen to you harass my guest the entire trip I would have left you at home." Kai's nose hovers just a hair away from Rowan's. His gaze squints as he focuses on his brother. Maybe I'm not the only one who wants to burn a hole into his soul...

"Calm down," Rowan tries to push his brother's hands off of him. Kai remains unmovable. "It's just a joke."

"It's. Not. Funny." Each syllable is firm.

"You're just saying this because the Wishing Spirit bit you and transferred some of its rage to you." Rowan brings his fists down, hitting Kai's elbows hard enough his brother drops him. He points his finger into his chest.

"Don't you try and look all big and bad to me. Give yourself another hour and you'll have withdrawals so bad I could blow you over like a piece of lint."

Muscles chord in Kai's jaw, a large vein bulging in his neck. He pulls his brother closer, finally letting their noses brush. I'd crack a joke about brotherly love if it wasn't for the way both their ears were turning red and I could feel the anger coming off of them in waves.

"Would you like to test your theory?" Kai finally manages.

Rowan arches back and laughs. "We're going to do this right now? Over a joke? Over her?"

Her.

I stand up, talking softer to Kai. "Just put him down."

"Listen to your *Cupcake*, Kai." Rowan teases.

Kai takes his time lowering his brother and letting go of the front of his shirt. Rowan watches with a daring smile and flattens down the wrinkles their spat has created.

"That's better," Rowan continues.

"Yeah, Kai, I can fight my own battles." I give Kai's bicep just the smallest squeeze before I whirl on his brother. I focus every ounce of frustration, fear, and outright anger at how life was handed to me and I channel it into my fist. My knuckles make contact with the sharp angle of Rowan's jaw.

Pain instantly blooms in my hand. Rowan grabs his cheek and takes a confused step back as I bite my lip and turn back to Kai. The blonde-haired prince is watching me with his brows lifted up to his hairline. Tears of surprise are welling along my eyelids and I shove my hand between my thighs as if their thickness could cuddle the pain away. Why does punching someone hurt so bad? It's supposed to hurt him not me!

"Damn, Briar!" Rowan scrubs at his face. "Why the hell would you do that?"

"To teach you a lesson," I groan.

A large grin finally breaks Kai's lips and he leans forward grabbing both of my shoulders. "You are bloody brilliant, Cupcake. Though, perhaps, with your human fragility we shouldn't go around punching Fae with Iron in their bones." Kai looks back up to Rowan. "You're lucky it wasn't my fist. It'd do you well to go find yourself some place to rest away from us. And next time don't try to talk her into giving you sexual favors for items that are a necessity. Or rather, you just don't ask for sexual favors."

Rowan rolls his eyes but ultimately listens. His boots kick at the ground as he works his way around us and heads for the back of the cave. He pulls an apple from his backpack and tosses it in the air a few times already moving on from the situation and no longer caring about the hit that didn't even leave a red mark on his face.

Kai shakes his head. "Let me see your hand."

I clench my teeth as I pull my hand from between my legs. In offering, I hold it up between us. My knuckles are a dark red and I'm reminded of my weakened state every time I bend my fingers for him.

"Well, you'll probably have a nice bruise but other

than that, no broken bones." Kai presses a gentle kiss to my knuckles. It stings when his lips brush my skin.

A sigh of relief is all I can respond with. The gesture of his kiss so sweet it reminds of something Lincoln would have done. They were brought up by the same people. Rowan must be the odd man out when it comes to their upbringing because his incessant flirting and lack of respect for other people's boundaries is really setting the tone for a less than pleasant friendship.

"So... we're going to sleep here?" I press my back to the cave wall and slide down to sitting, the hilt of the dagger digs into my side.

"Yes."

I flick my attention up to his face. "I want you to say 'Yeah', just one time for me."

"That's an odd request." He tilts his head to the side. The pink of his tongue slips out over his bottom lip before he tries. "Yeah."

It's much more attractive with his accent, I think. It must be my accent that makes it sound so uneducated.

"Yeah," he tries again this time grasping at my accent. "Yeah." He perfects the tone.

"It's nice not to be so formal all the time, huh?" I ask.

"I'm a prince. One day I'll be a king. I don't really do informal."

Kai paces a few feet in front of me, sending a weary glance to his brother. Rowan sits in the corner, chewing on his apple. He avoids our attention, finding something truly intriguing about the rock across from him. Kai slips his hands into his pocket. He looks down at me.

"You'll be safe tonight. I promise."

The temperature is steadily dropping with the setting sun and I'm suddenly very aware of the chill coating my once sweat dampened skin.

"I didn't pack a blanket," I confess.

"You won't need one."

Finally, Kai crosses his legs and squats down until he's sitting in front of me. He picks at his nails looking almost bashful. I squint trying to process if I should be worried that he's hitting on me now.

"What do you mean?"

"I can do this..." He reaches out and presses his fingers against my wrist.

Heat bubbles in my veins. Every rushing pulse pushes the heat through the rest of my body. It's hot but not scorching. Magic that doesn't burn but soothes... like a blanket. Even the wall behind me seems to soften.

I give him a lazy smile. "Are you trying to put me to sleep right now."

He leans to check the sun outside. If it's at all above the horizon the mountain has totally blocked it from our view. I can't even make out the tree tops or the ground that we made on our journey today. It's just black. Everything is dark.

I close my eyes. Dark. Everything is dark. Dark enough that I could just go to sleep. When he speaks, I only crack one eye for him.

"No, but you should rest because we'll be up bright and early tomorrow and I'm sure unlocking your powers is going to be some sort of trip for you."

"Uh-huh." I nod, closing my eyes, content to sleep against the wall. "I didn't know you had this sort of power."

"I've got all sorts of things that you don't know about me," he whispers.

ELEVEN

ZEVE

"WE'RE HERE!" Rowan calls.

"Where exactly is here?" I pull myself up, clambering, cautiously up the rocks. The higher we rise the less trees are sprouting. Dust has begun to fill the air, it clings to us like ash. I can even taste it, like burnt raw dirt, on my tongue.

"Does the seer live here?" I ask.

Rowan stops at the mouth of another cave. The entrance to it is so slender, I'm not sure that either of the Fae are going to be able to fit through. Even I'll need to suck in and crush my boobs against me to make it between that tiny opening.

"The seer lives here," Kai says mostly to the sky.

Dark clouds are forming around the mountain range. The flash of light and the following boom an eerie threat of what is to come. I pray it's just my own paranoia. This isn't foreshadowing. Right?

"Do we knock?" I swallow the lump in my throat.

Rowan offers me his hand on the final step I have to make up the landing he balances on. He holds my hand gently. I'd like to say it has something to do with the right hook I'd shared with him the day before. More likely though, it has to do with the conversation the two were having when I woke up. Not a minute after Rowan had trudged over to me looking like a child who'd just gotten grounded and apologized for his less than princely behavior. He promised not to ask for sexual favors anymore but insisted he couldn't turn off the flirting. 'It's just who he is as a person.'

I decided that the apology was enough and put the entire thing behind us. And sure enough, when I glanced down at my knuckles a healthy purple bruise covered the back of my hand. At least now I could admit to having punched royalty. That has to mean something, right?

Next on the list. Kill Queen Cordelia.

What a fucking leap.

Kai had chosen to watch us from behind. Mostly so that Rowan didn't get another chance to look at my ass. At no point when I turned back to Kai did I find him watching my rear-end. He's probably missing Jase. I miss Jase.

I chew on my nail thinking back to my cousin. It'd hardly been weeks since I'd seen him but it feels like years. It wouldn't be forever though, I reminded myself. And if our Fae genes had anything to do with it, we would have forever to live together.

Kai presses his face against the crack. He takes a deep breath in then pulls away quickly. "The seer lives here alright."

"Does it smell?" I ask carefully.

"I'm surprised you can't smell it from there. I've been catching whiffs of rotting meat and dead carcass since I got up on this little witch's front porch." Rowan waves his hand in front of his face.

I try to sniff again. I don't really smell much of anything. Probably, a good thing for now.

"Um, why would there be rotting meat or something dead?"

"It's pretty normal to bring some sort of a sacrifice for a seer. Not only does the blood help them to really conduct their sort of magic, they can live off the meat for a while and not need to leave their little holes to hunt." Kai bends, trying to get another angle to peer into the cave.

"What, uh... I really hate to ask this. What did we bring for a sacrifice?" My mouth feels immensely dry.

"Why do you think we brought Rowan?" Kai points at his brother.

"Ha, ha, ha. Very funny, asshole." Rowan throws a gentle punch at his brother. Kai fists it with a stern glance.

"Seriously, though?" I attempt to lean around the brothers to try and get a look at the dark cave. Hints of the meaty smell waft up to me as I try to ready myself for whatever sort of magical transformation is about to happen. Without a thought, my hands drift up and touch the amulet clasped around my throat.

All I can picture is this magical movie moment. My body will get picked up by a tornado of air, my arms and legs stretching behind my torso. Color will glow blindingly bright from the necklace as the seer chants some ancient language. In a snap everything will go dark... but then everything will be made new. I'll see things I couldn't before, smell things from farther distances, and get flooded with the gracefulness of the Fae.

At least that's what I'm guessing. I could be wrong.

"Seriously," Kai mocks my accent. "We don't need a sacrifice. She owes me a favor."

"She owes you... a favor? How do you get a seer in debt to you?"

"That's a story about a young Fae who did a lot of stupid things and found a friend who... also did a lot of stupid things."

Rowan crosses his arms, listening to his brother with a smirk. "Kai wasn't always such a good boy," he hums. "Now. Who's going first?"

"Briar is going alone." Kai nods.

"I'm what, now?" His words hit me in the chest, knocking the wind out of me.

"Neither Rowan or I can help you with this. This is between you and the seer. Tell her it's in fulfillment of my debt."

I touch the lip of the cave. The coming and going through the entrance has worn the rock smooth just in this one spot. Every other plane on the side of the volcano is bubbled. Black ash clings to my fingers as I pull away.

A flash of lightning makes light pour over the mountain range, the rumble of thunder quick to follow. I turn my face up to the sky. It's only taken minutes for the clouds to turn near black with the threat of a nasty storm.

Wind blows at my ponytail, sending my hair thrashing behind me. "Are you sure you don't want to come inside, even if only to avoid the storm?"

"This isn't for us to do," Rowan says loudly. "I agree with my brother even if I'm not entirely excited about standing out in the rain."

"You'll look like a drowned rat with those skinny little braids of yours." Kai says.

I can picture Rowan sopping wet. The short strands of hair around his face flattened against his skull and the few long strands braided behind him. He would truly look like a rat. I mean, I'd always considered the braids at the bottom of his hairline to be sort of like rat tails.

"Okay, I guess there isn't anything else for me to do but enter the cave." I clap my hands together.

And to work up the courage to you know... actually do it.

"Are you going?" Rowan says.

"Yes."

"Your legs aren't moving..." Kai reminds me.

Assholes.

I step forward. "Are you happy?"

"Very." Rowan leans against the mountainside.

A droplet of rain lands on the bare skin of my arm. It's cold and rolls gently down me, following the curve of my forearm. Another drop follows. It'll be pouring soon and I'm not sure I want to meet the seer soaked to the bone.

"Good luck with the storm," I toss to the two men as I push myself through the skinny entrance.

Stone brushes against my chest as I hold in all of my breath. The light from the day only travels so far once I'm inside. Rot fills the cave. Carcasses, bones, mounds of only what I can only assume is old flesh, are tossed here and there. The smell of it burns on the way to my lungs. I gag, feeling my stomach lurch at the sight.

Beyond that there is only more darkness. Even as I try to allow my eyes time to adjust, nothing becomes clearer. How far back will I need to travel to meet the seer?

I check my neck for good measure, reassured that the necklace hasn't suddenly disappeared. As I brush it, it thrums against my skin. I feel the beat of it travel inside of my chest. The metal around the stone warms slightly. All of it disappearing after just a few seconds.

It's as if it's calling out to like magic. The seer couldn't be too far away then.

"Hello?" I try, automatically feeling like the idiot girl in the beginning of a horror film. *See this... this is how people die, Briar.*

The blade that Kai gifted me bounces against my leg. It rests inside of a sheath that's also clearly borrowed. I pull it gently out and hold it in front of me as I descend where my sight is no longer of use. My feet shuffle against the dust covered floors, echoing through the cave.

Another 'hello' rises to my lips, but this time I resist the urge to call out. The seer might live in this cave, but I'd imagine other animals could live here too. Or other sacrifices she hasn't needed to kill yet. If the panther Kai hunted was as large as it was, how big are the bears? How big are other already large animals?

Picturing some dragon looking creature curled at the back of this cave does my anxiety few favors. Sweat gathers between my palm and the hilt of the knife. I tighten my grip on it, letting the gems dig into my skin.

"Do you really think that will do you any good?" A sensual voice whispers. The sound surrounds me in such a way I can picture her both in front of and behind me.

I point the knife anyway, spinning in a circle. "Are you the seer?"

"Is that who you want me to be?" she says even softer.

What if it's another Wishing Spirit? Or some new monster I have yet to learn about?

"My name is Briar. Briar Anders." I swallow. "I'm here asking a favor to fill the debt of Kai Ziko."

"Yyyeeesssss," The sound is long, drawn out, and all too eerily similar to that of a snake's hiss. "I can smell my old friend on you. If only he would come in so we can catch up."

"He said this is something I have to do on my own."

No matter how I try, my attention dances in the dark

without any one spot to focus. The Seer is neither here nor there... if she's even a physical being at all. I think back to Lylix and her ghostly form. Is that what this Seer is too? A ghost? Or is she more like Lincoln? More Fae than anything.

"And what is it that you've come here to do?"

"Isn't that something a seer would already know?" I blurt. I bite my lip hoping I hadn't offended her. Remember... I need her help.

"You are young," the Seer laughs. "Your young tongue has yet to be tamed, I see. But I will indulge you. Miss Briar Anders, I've waited many years for your arrival. You've climbed my mountain and found the courage to enter my cave where your senses are of little use..." She sniffs the air loudly. "You have an object of magic."

"I do."

"I remember the piece. I also remember the frantic young girl, whom you so resemble, begging me to deliver you and hide you amongst the humans. You were too powerful from birth to walk among them and not be noticed." Even in the dark I imagine the Seer is smiling. "Now you're back to undo all my work."

"You met my mother?" My hands shake. I lower the knife, still holding it in my hand.

"She was a kind woman, too sweet for her own good. Your strength... the whit of it... that is of your father."

"I struggle to have any sympathy for my father who had my mother beheaded," I admit out loud.

"Don't let your turmoil stew like that. It will turn

your soul black." The strings of the Seer's voice pull from all around. Her unidentified position narrowing to just a few feet ahead of me. In a single blink, a soft glow begins to fill the cave. A glow radiates off the seer's skin.

Only with her light am I able to make out her features. Soft brown skin without imperfection, large almond shaped eyes filled with uncapped knowledge, full pouting lips, and dark brown hair that hangs down her back, stopping at the back of her knees are all features that inspire an endless youth. Now without the darkness, I can see many more skeletons. Not all of them are animals.

"You can put your knife away now, Briar." She lifts a delicate brow, that is hardly seen under the blunt cut of bangs across her forehead.

I nod, doing as she says. I try to breathe through my mouth to avoid the smell in the air, and I wipe the sweat from my palms against my jeans.

"Give me the necklace." The Seer holds out her hand.

I reach behind my neck, undoing the clasp and letting the gem and metal gather in my hand. "Will it hurt? Getting my powers back."

"Oh, that depends entirely on your mother, Dear."

"How so?" I stretch out my arm, reluctantly. The Seer waits patiently until I finally let go of the necklace.

She smiles, giving me the full view of every pointed tooth. With a diet like hers I would expect her teeth to be lined with red, pointed and dangerous, similar to the teeth of the Wishing Spirit. But they aren't. Her smile is shining perfectly, just like everything else about her.

"I may have helped seal your powers into this priceless family heirloom, but it was your mother who created any challenges that you may face. I'd assume it's something to make it much harder for anyone else to have the ability of stealing your power."

She lifts the necklace to her eye, examining the stone. "Maybe you'll need that knife after all." Her smile grows wider. "You'll need to relax." The seer begins. She clutches the stone, my powers, the one thing I have of my mothers, to her chest.

"It turns out that I'm not great at doing that." I start. "Do you, uh, have a name?"

Her large black eyes tick up to my face. "Zeve."

"Zeve." I repeat. "How do we...? I'm ready to start."

Zeve walks around me, eyeing me from head to toe. The silky, brown dress, somehow unaffected by the ragged environment around her, swishes around her knees. It's almost as mesmerizing to watch as the way in which she walks with such confidence and grace.

"I'll open the door for you and the rest is up to you." Zeve steps up so that her bare feet touch my boots. I marvel at the cleanliness of her skin against the debris of the cave floor. More magic? Does a highly sought out seer, like her, have an end to her magic?

"Okay, I—"

Zeve pushes the large stone, warm from her grasp, against my forehead. Heat travels against my skull then down through my body, burning like boiling water pumping in my veins. White light explodes behind my eyelids. My intake of breath is weak, a raspy gasp that claws all the way down my throat and into my lungs. Is it the power from within the stone? Is it the pain of the magic?

My knees buckle, slamming against the ground with a loud crack. The light, the pain, the screaming heat dies away with every heartbeat. I clutch Kai's knife at my belt.

"Open your eyes." Zeve's voice echoes through a space large and empty.

I open my eyes only to find sand. So much sand. Endless desert.

And no one and nothing in sight.

TWELVE

GULLIBLE

Wind tears at my clothes, pushing them flush against my body as I try and push forward. It howls in my ears. It's the only noise in the absence of Zeve's voice. I strain to hear anything more. I'm expectant of the sound of animals in the distance. There's nothing but the shift of my boots as I take a step forward.

I open my mouth to make a sound, maybe to call out, but dry sand gathers on my tongue brought by the continuous gusts around me. The worry of being without water makes my body already crave a drink, even if I'm not dehydrated.

Far ahead, beyond what I believe to be flat land, I can see where it changes to the bumpy texture of rising sand mounds before the rise of wind-worn rocks. The sun has no end here. There are no trees for shade or even a spot of clouds in the blue sky above.

It's just me and the sun.

I lift one foot and step forward. The world rotates, the 'hello' just a passing thought.

I sink as water rises over my body in a foaming wave. The desert scene being replaced with the expanse of a sea without land in sight. Catching air, I brace myself as the wave pushes me under and a current pulls my body backwards.

Dust plumes into the air around me, hot sand clinging to my now damp skin. My hair drips against my forehead magnifying the sun that beats down.

Holy, fucking fuck. What was that? Where was that?

There is an urge to wipe the salt water from my eyes but when I lift my hands I know it'll do me little good. I clap my hands together trying to brush away the dirt.

What kind of magic has my mother guarded this place with? Better yet, how am I going to find my magic?

Standing, I spin in a circle hesitant to take a step in any real direction. Desert. I take a deep breath and step forward.

My clothes drag me heavily under the rocking of the ocean top. I only glimpse at the stormy sky and fluffy black clouds. They've strung together in the oddest fashion, moving with an unnatural speed. I want to see more. I need to see more.

But my head goes under. My boots are like anchors tied around my feet. Down and down I go. Bubbles edge their way over my face as trapped air finds its escape. I reach, tugging at my laces, and pushing out of my one boot, then the next. I kick. Under me, my legs push and pump myself toward the surface, my arms propelling as they force the water down and my body up towards the sky.

Inside my chest, my lungs burn. It's reminiscent of the magic that brought me into this world. I have to wonder... if that's all it is now. It's not that my body has been deprived of the oxygen it needs or that I've been underwater for too long. It's that this entire place, the desert, the ocean, it's all magic.

It's all magic. And it fucking burns!

Under the water is darkness. Salt stings in my eyes as I look for the surface with little light to offer from above. Air finally hits me. Water slicking every strand of hair flat to my head.

Lighting strikes with a flash across the sky. The clouds glow with it. I follow their curve trying to make out their depictions like a child guessing the shapes as different animals. Only these are most certainly letters.

Just as quickly as the storm offered me visibility of the clouds the water takes it away. Water slaps against my skin pushing my body away and my face sideways into the ground. The hard, sand covered ground.

Damn it all!

I cough water, that I'd inhaled in the punch, out into the dust. Groaning as I let my head rest, I breathe heavily. The rocks in the distance cast the only shadow for miles against each other. I blink at them.

The shadows curl like a snake then pitch like upside down mountains. This better not be a mirage. I try sitting up but the shadow shifts into nothingness, again. So I lower myself to the dirt, letting my breath send the small particles into clouds.

S.

W.

I.

M.

SWIM. FUCKING SWIM. The desert is telling me what to do when I fall into the ocean? So there is a word in the cloud. Context clues. Context clues. I chant to myself. So maybe my mother was banking on me being semi-smart and less on brawn. But even this... this is almost too easy.

But there isn't anything else to do. I roll my body forward one time and tumble from the sand back into the ocean. The water claws at me with its frozen fingers, so drastically different from the dunes of the dry sand. Another wave is already growing in height not too far away.

I look past it, knowing if I don't start swimming soon I'll be drug back to where I started. But I need the command first. Squinting up at the clouds I hope the darkness doesn't play tricks on me. They swirl and curve so smoothly I wonder how I was able to make out words in the first place.

JUMP.

Jump. Next I need to jump. But now... as I see the wave heading straight for me... I need to swim. *Swim, Briar, swim!* Something inside of me cheers and I slap my palm down and break the surface of the sea and surge forward.

My shirt catches on thorns, my hand hanging over the edge of rock. Wild flowers, in pale yellows and royal purples shoot up in front of my face. I drag my hands under me and push myself up, getting my feet under me. My sock feet—the pretty boots now tragically long gone. Water gathers in a puddle around me, making the brush I'd landed that's squashed down to the earth sparkle.

There is an end to the wild here. A long meadow dotted with blooms comes to a point and abruptly disappears at the edge of a cliff where I stand. I swallow, hard.

Jump. This bitch wants me to jump.

Maybe I shouldn't refer to my mother as a bitch, but goddamn.

A tremble travels through my legs. My vision blurring at the edges. There could be sweat building on my forehead and gathering in my palms but the ocean clings to me so fiercely I can't decipher the difference. I lean as far as I can, looking down over the edge. It's nothingness. It's rock that falls into darkness with no sounds of running water below. I have no guess for what comes next but I know that I can't leave this spot until I find the same direction.

I turn, my gaze running over anything and everything. The sky is clear, the sun not near as demanding as the desert. I'm trying to make letters out of petals and flower stems. They'd gather into beautiful bouquets but they don't spell anything out.

With a frustrated hiss, I ring out my shirt. I crouch down, pinching at my pant-legs to dispel any water that I can. Grass is bent at odd angles from my entrance to the meadow, and if the decision was up to me this would be a perfect spot to hide a word.

A great *caw* carries over to me as a bird flies across the sky. The first I've seen of life in either of the three scenarios. My attention is quickly drawn to it as I watch it circle down closer to me. It has long dark feathers that grow to a light shade of brown closer to its face. Its beak shines the off-white color of bones.

Clamped between its jaws dangles another animal, limp in death. A tail hangs down, long and skinny, reminiscent of a rat's. I frown at the sight. Frowning more deeply the closer the bird comes. I don't move though, because where would I go? Back into the ocean? On to the next place with no direction of how to move on?

I mean, 'swim', was pretty self-explanatory but 'jump'.... no sane person is going to find themselves at a cliffs edge and automatically think 'I should jump.'

The bird opens its beak and caws again around the carcass of the mangled animal. It chomps down splitting the animal in two. One end falls from the sky and splatters against the ground at my feet. Hot blood splatters against my pant legs.

I shriek. Or more so I groan and try not to think about it too hard. Blood still has a way of taking me back to Cordelia's castle. Of haunting me with the memory of

Harley and everyone else that's suffered at their queen's hands. In a way, it gives me new strength.

I look down. Whatever the animal had once been, it no longer is. All that's left is a skin bag that holds crumpled bones and torn unidentifiable features. I want to wipe the splatter from my pants. Glancing at the plants around me none of them have leaves wide enough to use as napkins. Even wiping it away with my hands would be better.

Moving to drag my hands over my shin, I quickly stop when I realize. Three swirling letters written in an eloquent cursive drip down my leg.

LIE.

To who? What about?

I nod to myself. Okay, I can do this. Now, all I need to do is jump. So I stand, leaving the blood as it is on my pants. The earth tilts in a dizzying way as I look down into the abyss I'm about to leap into. I squeeze my eyes tight, bend my knees, and jump.

Air rushes by, sending my hair above my head as I fall. My feet land together on a worn grass walkway, my hair swinging from the momentum of my landing. I'd slammed against the earth so hard that pain shoots up my legs. Voices carry around and I look over my shoulder to watch a pair of people strolling toward me.

The moon is high in the sky and beyond the couple are lights and cheering Fae. I turn and find a brilliant mansion and a glowing garden with a sparkling Reminints tree. The Shadow Court. My father's memory. Or is it my mother's?

The friends laugh as they pass me, giving me weird looks as they carry on their conversation.

"You're so gullible. Always doing everything you're told." One slaps the other on the shoulder turning them away from me and the judgment they try to pass on. I'm sure I look insane to them. I'm more surprised though that they can see me.

"I'm just following my commands," they whine in response.

The friend shakes their head. "Stop. Next time they try to tell you to do something, do the opposite. I dare y— oh! It's the king."

The couple bows together. King Rihst storms by them without acknowledging their presence. He stomps right up to me. There is anger in his dark eyes. Still, I marvel at him. The father I never had. There are patches of red in the beard that grows on his chin, his skin is flushed over his cheeks, and though his ears lift to a point at the top it's remarkable how they stick off his head just as mine do.

"Who are you?" He demands stopping in front of me.

"Me?" I point to myself and look around as if he could be talking to anybody else.

"You." He narrows his gaze.

"Briar Anders."

Oh shit. I was supposed to lie. I remind myself.

His eyes soften but all other judgment and fury still

remain in his features. King Rihst lifts his chin. "Why are you here?"

Lie. Say a lie.

"I've just come for the fair." I point behind me to the merriment and games just down the small sloping hill.

He sighs, his lip curling in disgust. "I think you need to go for a walk." And he clamps his hand on my shoulder and pushes me. His strength propels me forward.

"No!" I cry with confusion as the blinding sun replaces the midnight moon. My father's image, the familiarness of the Shadow Court, the twinkle of lanterns, all fades like a dream.

I tilt my head up to the sky, screaming with frustration. I don't know what to think. I don't know what to do. Lowering myself to the sand, I lay sideways as I was when the ocean brought me back with a violent cruelty. My shoulders shake with a shuddering breath.

How? How am I going to do this? How?

I want to scream. I want to throw my fists into the dirt and kick my legs like a toddler. Never once did I ask for a hard life, I didn't ask to be an orphan or ask to have to find my way back to the magic that belongs to me in the first place. Yet here I am. These are the cards that I've been dealt. And if I don't fight, I could die. Shadow Fae will die.

Cordelia Nightwaters *should* die.

The only reprieve from the sun is cast by the rocks. It still spells out *swim*. I don't need the reminder with the taste of the ocean still stuck to my tongue. I fist my hand and hit the ground just once with a growl. It's all I allow myself before I stand and step into the wicked waves.

This time I don't pay attention to the waves. I don't look to the clouds. Tropical air, cooled only by the storm that rages above, fills my lungs. I surge forward fighting the waters as I arch my arms over my head and then send them forcefully below the dark surface.

I stumble forward into the meadow. Broken weeds and stems catch on my wet socks. Behind me I hear the flapping of wings. The blood that was splattered on my pant legs before, now gone. Even the weeds where my body had fallen the first time are no longer flattened against the earth. It's as if I'd never been here at all.

Run and jump. Jump from the fucking cliff, Briar.

This is the worst part, in my opinion, the purposeful jumping. Next to not having any clue what the hell I'm supposed to be doing here. Still, I leap. Even if I can't bring myself to open my eyes until I'm standing in the grass once more.

It's here. Whatever it is, it's here in this scene with my father where I'm going wrong. I'm not answering him correctly.

Context clue. Context clues.

A familiar breeze passes carrying the voices of the fair. The voices of the friends that bump against each other as they walk, talk, and laugh. I can see as they sway this time that perhaps they've visited the Reminints tree far too many times this evening. I look beyond them to the lighters flicking. Something somewhere has to tell me what to do.

The meadow, the blood splatter, told me to lie. Maybe saying my name in truth had been where I'd gone wrong. What false name should I give? Does it matter?

Nothing in the movement of the Fae, nothing in the lights and fun at the distance, nothing on their clothing so much as suggests a word or a prompt.

It was my father's last sentence that suggested what I should do in the desert. "You need to go for a walk." Replays in my mind. And I listened.

Maybe I should just listen.

Together the pair chuckles. Both their gazes travel wearily down my clinging, wet clothing. They judge but don't give me enough of their attention to put a pause to their conversation.

"You're so gullible. Always doing everything you're told." The first grabs his friends' shoulder, pointing them away from me.

"I'm just following my commands," they complain.

The friend shakes their head. "Stop. Next time they try to tell you to do something, do the opposite. I dare y— oh! It's the king."

I'm so gullible. They're talking to me.

My mistake is doing everything I'm told. So... I should disobey? Do the opposite?

King Rihst is already hustling toward me, his robe flying behind him. What does he tell me to do? I'm racking my brain thinking back to the first conversation. He asks me some questions but his only command is to walk. So what if I didn't walk in the desert? What if I didn't swim in the ocean? What if I didn't jump from the cliff?

What if... I didn't lie?

Two polished boots stop in front of me. He disapproves of my attire, so clearly, his scowl only deepens as he takes in my ragged state. King Rihst balls his hands up, keeping his arms straight as his side. It reminds me of the frustration and the way I wanted to throw a fit like a child.

"Who are you?" he spits.

"Briar Anders," I say with certainty. I'm telling the truth. I won't follow the commands of the amulet any longer.

The scrunch of his brow lifts ever so slightly. No other tensions leave his body, still he lifts his chin. "Why are you here?"

"I've come for my powers."

Rihst brings one of his large hands up to his mouth. His eyes shine as he watches me with a new sort of scrutiny. "Are you," he clears his throat, "Are you the child of Amelia Nightwaters?"

To hear Cordelia's last name is a shock. Though I suppose it's really the king's last name that she's then carried. Slowly, I nod my head.

"Say it out loud," he whispers, closing his eyes. "The magic won't work if you don't say it out loud."

"Yes. I am your daughter. I am the child of Amelia Nightwaters."

He covers his entire face now. A loud whimper caught in his grasp. I give him a moment, trying to calm the shock of my own body. Goosebumps travel over my skin as he lowers his hands, showing me the torment that lives within him. His lip quivers.

"Briar Anders." He tastes the name. "We've waited a long time for you."

SPELLBOUND

KING RIHST STEPS CLOSER, lifting his hands then dropping them with uncertainty back to his sides. He cocks his head. It's clear he is fiddling, not really knowing what to do with his own body. It's odd for me to see. Kings, as I've known of them, are quite certain of themselves.

"May I?" he asks, his voice hardly louder than the breeze, lifting his hands to my face.

"Yes." I still.

Carefully, he runs his thumb over the apples of my cheeks, cupping his hands on either side of my face. He watches me, then slowly brushes back my water logged hair. "Let me fix that." He waves his hand and I can feel the wetness lifting away from my skin. My hair pulls over my head only until he drops his hand again and it falls back to my shoulder in loose curls.

"You look so much like your mother." His strong arms wrap around my shoulders, tugging me into his chest. My arms remained pinned at my sides. My father holds me tightly. Slowly, I let myself breathe him in and relax against him.

"I'm sorry," he whispers into my ear. "I'm sorry I didn't protect myself from that witch's spell. I'm sorry I couldn't protect your mother. I'm sorry I never got to see you grow up."

I clench my teeth. Tears well in my eyes. I try my best to hold them in, to keep myself from the place of vulnerability that still feels raw and wounded. But as he squeezes me tighter, as he presses the lightest kiss to my temple, my body shakes a release, a quiet sob. A few tears spill over my eyelids and dry on my cheeks. I step away from him, wiping them away.

I have nothing to say. Was it okay that all of these things happened to him, to my mother, to me? No. Was he in control enough to have prevented them from happening? No. So, I can't bring myself to accept the apology but I bob my head in acknowledgment.

"Come now." He offers his arm. "Let me take you to your mother."

Looping my arm in his, the skin on my face feels tight from the drying tears. The king walks but he doesn't take his eyes off of me, staring like he has to memorize my face.

"Gods, I can't get over how much you look like Amelia." He sniffles. "You're beautiful. And currently very human, I see. We'll need to fix that."

My father and I move toward the garden. When I

step onto the stone path that loops between the plants, I realize not only has he dried my feet, but my boots are on and laced back up. I look down, in admiration of his magical abilities.

He truly is a powerful, powerful Fae clearly.

"Thank you," I say.

"You'd catch a cold running around dressed like that all soaking wet. It's the least I could do. I will add that the quick change of scenery was all your mother's idea. She's a brilliant one, I'd say. And I have her to thank for bringing me here in my death."

"Excuse me?"

King Rihst laughs as I subtly lean away. "We are very much real, Briar. At least our souls, not so much the magic that is currently making up what you see as our physical bodies." He brushes away the waving strands of the Reminints tree. "When your mother had you taken from her womb, she had your Fae half removed and placed for safe keeping in what I'm told is my mother's necklace. But she also had my soul and hers tied to the very same piece."

"Even though she knew that you were putting her to death?" I chew on my lip watching the moon above us.

"She loves me as I love her and she saw the deception for what it was, in thanks to our dearest friend Lylix."

"So, you're real?"

"Mostly, real." A female voice says with certainty.

My attention snaps to my mother. Her curls are brought up on top of her head, making it easier to see the blush of her cheeks, and the joy in her gaze. She holds her arms out for me and walks toward me. My father lets me go. I stumble forward and crash into her arms. Her sweet scent washes over me, the lavender smell that the Wishing Spirit had tricked me with. It's indubitable now. She's alive now.

Everything is comfortable in her arms. Homey even. Is this what a true mother is supposed to feel like? I suppose I've seen glimpses of this love in fleeting moments with new foster families. Those moments always came to an end. Does a mother's love truly ever have an end? Here it doesn't feel like it.

"I don't understand how this is you, really you." I hold her at arm's length. She looks as she did in my father's memory. Young. Too young to die. "You look so much younger than me."

"I mean... I am. I was, physically. My soul is older now." She reaches a hand up to run over my cheek, much like my father had. "This place is only held together by the ties of your magic. Once we gift it to you, we'll be gone. Our souls released to the after world."

"You've just been here? This whole time? My whole life?" Living inside the silly necklace that I'd stuffed in my jewelry box on top of my dresser and swore I'd never wear because it was so gaudy. I gesture toward this false world, the night of the fair that has been frozen into an eternity. "Is the night always the same?"

"Yes." The queen guides me to the bench she had

risen from, offering me a seat. The king glides behind us, content with watching us interact.

"Sometimes it's maddening," he adds.

"But mostly, we're just thankful for all these years we were still able to spend together. We've waited for you, Briar." The queen holds both my hands in hers. "We only have a short minute together but I couldn't move on without getting to meet our child. I've mourned for many years never getting the chance to watch you grow or hold you and rock you to sleep. There were so many motherly moments I've missed out on but it's all worth it to know that it's kept you safe."

Safe. I'm not safe. My half-sister wishes me dead, she's killed innocents on her hunt to end my life, to protect her throne. But I suppose in some ways... what she did... it got me here. I'm alive. I've found my home. I've found my people. Is that *enough*?

"Cordelia," I start, "holds the crown. She's terrorizing the people, killing their babies, killing innocent Shadow Fae that find themselves in her court after wandering in from the human world. I've got to stop her. I've got to make a claim for the throne."

King Rihst looks down at his feet. He wrings his hands together without speaking.

"You do us proud to seek justice as you do," Queen Amelia speaks softly, her eyes sparkling with her smile. "Cordelia was born with trickery. She was bred by her mother to one day take the crown and make their blood-line royal. But..." She looks up to her husband. "She was once a little girl who loved her dad. And despite it all, he loved her too. This is a hard topic for him. Understandably."

"She's technically blood. But if I don't end her, she'll end me."

"I know." He sits gingerly down next to me on the bench. "What happens in your world now is out of our control. It's past our time and we have no say. I know this. So I won't try to sway you in any sort of direction. I found my death at her hands and I still can't bring myself to hate her. For you, though, it's different."

Folding my hands into my lap, I fiddle with my thumbs and pick at my fingernails. King Rihst may have love for Cordelia in his heart, but I do not. We may share a father but that's where the similarities end.

"Tell me about your life." My mother sits up straighter, her tone full of curiosity and more certainly a sense of hope.

"Well, I was working...in the human world, as a teacher's assist before I stumbled into The Shadow Court—"

"A teacher!" The king exclaims. "What a wonderful profession!"

I haven't the heart to correct him. I was only a teacher's aide. Would they even know the difference?

"I mean it's a lot different than being a king or queen," I laugh nervously. "But I ran into Lincoln and he—"

"A boy." My mother gasps, holding her chest and sending an excited look toward my father.

"A man. Who is like a hundred years older than me... but that isn't the point." It's hard to stifle my laugh. "Lincoln helped me figure out who I was."

"He sounds lovely."

"Are you seeing him?" My father's brows pinch together.

"No, not exactly—"

"Rihst," Amelia swats at him. "Don't judge the boy you've never met."

I bite my lip to hide my growing smile. A thousand questions sit heavy on my tongue, that I can't bide any longer.

"What... What sort of powers will I have?" I blurt in the small lull in conversation.

My mother scoops my hand into hers, her skin like velvet. She interlaces our fingers and gives my hand a small squeeze. "Well, you'll grow stronger, become faster, your senses will be more developed and more able to focus. You'll have the royal bloodline to thank for most of your abilities to will things into existence. To touch minds to some extent."

"Like a seer?"

Like Lincoln? I want to ask but don't.

"Seers have the ability to see into one's future and one's past. They know all that was and is to come. So, unfortunately, not like a seer. And it won't work on any Fae that has had practice in guarding their minds. But it will work on lesser Fae, other creatures that are unguarded, and most certainly on humans."

I can't imagine having that sort of control. What would I even do with it? Why would I truly want to use it? Power in the human world only corrupts. Will it ruin me too when I become Fae?

"Will it hurt?"

"Would I hurt you?" she says in a hushed tone.

Truthfully, I can't answer that. I don't know her. I know of her. I have a small idea of what she was like and now that she *is,* I know that she'll only be around for a short period of time.

"I don't want to rush it. I've wanted my whole life to know who my parents were. Then I found you... and you were dead. This is my only chance to talk with you, I don't want to let you go."

The king laughs, dryly, looking to my mother for direction. She gives him a soft smile. Gently, she drapes her arm over my back, her fingertips rest on my father's shoulder and she pats him.

"There is a time limit once you've found your way to us. I put most of my magic into making the realms you have to find your way through to get to us and even then, only someone who is truly honest, someone who truly shares my blood, could lift the veil into this world that we live in. When your father was pulled away, called by the magic to fulfill his duty to the stone, I knew the time was near. I prayed that it was you and not someone else who had gotten their hands on the necklace. These powers are for you and no one else. I'd never let them through." She sighs. "But because so much effort was put into that, our current state is fragile. We only have a few minutes."

"I can feel the spells unraveling and time slipping away." King Rihst says, staring off into the distance. When my mother speaks again, it snaps him out of his haze and turns back to me.

"We need to give you your powers and we need to do it now."

"I have so much to say. So much to ask." My voice is a weak whine. "I don't know where to start."

"Oh, honey. I'm just glad to have seen you. Truly seen you." My mother gathers me in another hug, pressing the perfect skin of her cheek against mine. "It's a mother's dream to see her children grow. But seeing you now... that's satisfactory."

"We've had over twenty years to wonder what you turned out like, what you looked like. You got so much of your mother I'm not sure that it's fair." My father points out.

"That just means, I've finally won the bet. I didn't forget about it!" She laughs.

"I'll make sure to kiss you good before it all ends."

My heart fills with joy, listening to their innocent banter. It's easy to imagine in this moment, that I'd grown up in that mansion listening to them bicker and flirt. That would have been a lovely childhood.

"Don't dwell on what cannot be undone." Amelia turns back to me. She stands, smooths her dress and holds out her hand. As she is, in the physical form that barely lived in her twenties, she looks like she could be my sister. Or my friend. It's harder to picture her as a mother, who at the age of her soul should resemble someone with grey in their hair and laugh lines around their mouth and in the crinkle of their eyes.

"May I have your hand? I think it's time." She keeps her voice firm, without wavering, a testament to her strength. Still, her hands tremble and her chest rises and falls with rapid breaths. "Rihst," she reminds my father.

He stands and offers a hand. "One hand please."

I place one hand in each of theirs. Their palms are smooth and uncalloused, which could be in the makings of their false physical bodies or simply because they were both royalty and never had to do much laboring.

"I love you." Amelia looks into Rihst eyes.

"I love you." He smiles, genuinely back.

They both grip my hands a little tighter. Eventually, they look back down at me. Born from them, half this amazingly brave woman, half this strong leader who bore faults that were not just his own until the day he was murdered.

"I've always loved you." My mother's voice cracks. She brings her free hand up, gently touching her lips. "I promised myself I wasn't going to cry. This is a happy moment. This is what we've waited so long for."

"It's okay." I offer the measly bit of comfort. My eyes still sting as if I could break down at any moment. I'm holding myself together for now, but that effort is brittle and could easily be broken.

"Regret nearly killed me several times in my physical life. But I never regretted creating a child with your mother. I've never regretted you. I love you. Now it's time that you go get that crown. Get what is rightfully yours." He bends down, flipping my hand, and presses a kiss to my palm.

"Close your eyes, Briar." Queen Amelia whispers. "Our time is nearly gone."

I obey, letting my shoulders fall away from my ears. Their grips grow warmer, their voices a soft chant of a language I don't know in the back of my mind. The strong scent of decay and lavender fills my nose. Rain beats against the walls that surround me and a flash of lightning makes the back of my eyelids appear red for a minute.

I close my fist, their hands gone. The voice in the back of my head, the chanting unrecognizable being, continues then slows only a foot away from me. My eyes snap open.

Everything's gone. My parents are gone. My back arches, my body changing, and an untamed cry splits the air.

I WON'T SAY I'M IN LOVE

I AWAKE SURPRISED at the softness of the cushions below me and the warmth of the blankets thrown over me. Fuzzy grey and white pelts are draped over my body, tucked underneath my chin. The hair tickles against my cheeks. A hand holds mine, their thumb stroking slowly over my skin. I can hear their breathing, not quite able to open my eyes.

But I'm back. The Iron Court welcomes me so sweetly.

The image of my mother flashes through my thoughts. It's followed quickly by the sight of my father kissing my hand as Kai had done many times.

"Get what is rightfully yours." Replays in his deep baritone voice. It makes my heart pound in my chest. It's all I can hear. It's all I can think.

Get what is rightfully yours. Get what is rightfully yours. Get what is rightfully yours.

I gasp, throwing myself into a sitting position. Both hands grab for my chest, for my heart that threatens to break through its cage. The blankets fall to a heap in my lap.

"You okay, Cupcake?" Kai says softly. He stands next to the bed, his hand hovering but not touching my back. "You're not alone." He reminds me.

I turn to stare at him. He's much cleaner than I remember him on the trip, his hair loose and still wet from a shower. Instead of the unfitted travel clothes he'd donned, he's back in his traditional suit with colorful embroidery. He offers a kind smile.

"I'm okay, Pudding." I try, my returned grin a little weak. Blood rushes to my head. The level floors of my room tip and turn, spinning in blurring circles. I lean into his hand behind me, remembering the Spirit's bite.

"Your wound!" I shout thinking about how the black blood had made his clothing stick to his skin.

Gently, he pulls his arm away and holds it for me to examine, pushing his sleeve up. "Seer fixed me up. I'm fine. Maybe you should lay back down?"

"Briar?" A raspy voice says.

My hair flies around me as I snap my attention to the familiar voice. I push both hands against the mattress to steady myself. Butterflies build inside my stomach, an excitement that swells inside of me. My cheeks automatically flush.

"Lincoln?"

He's dressed similarly to Kai, his tailored pants a

more muted tone and without a jacket or fancy design. Lincoln pulls himself away from the tall purple tinted window, his attention shifting between me and his brother.

I look down at my hand, realizing that in my effort to steady myself, I've taken Kai's hand again. Kai still watches me with gentleness, unbothered by his brother. Even though my head spins slightly, I pull both my hands into my lap and intertwine them. My fingers are longer, more delicate, my nails suddenly perfectly manicured.

"I'm different." The words are a shock. As if the recognition of it alone is a rubber band, something snaps inside of my brain. It ticks so hard I press against my temples with a groan.

Then I can hear it. I can hear it all. Lincoln's heartbeat. Kai's heartbeat. The sound of the blood rushing through their veins. In the halls, guards shift at their posts, mumbling quietly to each other. I can't make out what they say, but the second I focus on it it's like I'm part of their conversation.

My eyes grow wide as I look around the room. If I thought color was vibrant before... it's somehow deeper now. More meaningful. Lincoln's warm and musky scent lingers in the room, it mingles with Kai's, less rugged, fresh smell.

I pat myself, feeling my body, working my way up to my ears to find that they've stretched to a point. Yes... that is it. The seconds when I found myself inside that stupid cave on top of the volcano with Zeve, I wasn't in pain... I was being stretched. Even my legs feel a tad longer now, and I am already tall for a woman as it is.

"I'm sure it will take a moment to get used to." Kai draws his hand back into his lap and leans in the chair that sits next to the bed.

"Have you been here this whole time?" I ask him.

"Carried you back and waited for you to wake. You're my guest, my friend, I owe you as much."

"And you?" I turn back to Lincoln. Seeing his wide frame in person again, makes it almost painful to stay where I am. I'd imagined letting him circle me within his arms, letting our bodies line up in the way that they so perfectly do.

"Your mind went blank. I couldn't hear anything." His lips press into a thin line and he takes a step closer. "I came as soon as I could and found you... like this."

"Let me help you up," Kai offers. "I'm sure you'll find the world much different now that your sight has much improved."

"Do I look different?"

"Same Briar we all know and love." Kai smirks. "No, you didn't suddenly turn into a fairytale princess."

"I don't believe you." I laugh.

In my peripheral, Lincoln cringes but quickly masks it by running his hand down his face. Dark stubble has grown on his chin, not long enough to be called a beard but not clean enough to be bare.

If I did transform into some sort of princess, Fae being, then I'd expect that my body wouldn't feel so exhausted right now. Perhaps that's normal considering I just went through some sort of crazy change from totally human to partially Fae. Is there even a normal to compare this to? How often did Shadow Fae get their magic half stripped from them?

I place both my feet on the floor. My boots and the well-worn socks are long since gone. Has someone cleaned me? Dressed me? I glance at my body, worked into a simple red bra and matching panty set connected by only a few straps. I suppose this should be the least shocking thing considering the Fae don't have many boundaries and Lincoln's put me in and out a few outfits at this point. Still the tips of my ears burn.

With the first few steps, Lincoln moves toward me but slows when he realizes Kai's already there. The Prince hovers, holding his hands out ready to catch me should my body give out.

"Relax," I tell them both. "I gained powers, I didn't somehow get new legs." Even if they do shake a little with each step.

"Just a precaution." Kai continues to hold his hands out.

Lincoln's steps stop, his boots firmly planting to the ground, and his arms fold across his chest. He watches me, all emotions wiped clean from his face.

There is a mirror just inside the bathroom. I don't bother to hide my very bare backside as I drag myself over to the other room. Bright white light turns on in a flash as I enter. My eyes take no time to adjust and I realize... I could see the room clearly before the light even turned on.

I grab the mirror and pull myself toward it. My hair falls over my shoulders, not even slightly tousled from the long sleep I'd just awoken from. The strands perfectly align with one another, the honey hues of the brown appearing much more *gold*. Even my lips looked stained with some sort of color and my skin is that much clearer.

Small points of blue clasp over my shoulder. I squint at them wondering if the lingerie is multicolored. Looking over my shoulder, I give the mirror my back. My lungs fill with the rush of air and I almost jump away from the mirror entirely. It's not lingerie. It's... it's wings.

Stretched membranous blue wings glitter in the light. They're tucked flat against my back and curve down over my hips I quickly realize. With the thought, they shudder, a foreign feeling that's almost outside of my body all together. The edges peel up from my shoulders and off of my hips floating behind me. Almost as if I'm moving an arm or a leg but shaky. More like... I'm learning how to walk.

They flap in small strokes behind my back. The movement isn't smooth, every sway of the wings looks more like a twitch or a jerk.

"You said that I look the same!" I shout. I tuck a strand of hair behind my ears and stare at the pointed edges, still baffled by my wings. "I look a thousand times different."

Maybe it's the outfit but... I totally look taller. I feel taller.

Kai pokes his head in, stepping aside to make room for Lincoln who follows. Lincoln's arms are still crossed over his chest as he slouches in the doorframe.

"Your ears have changed." Kai points a finger at me.

I huff and lunge forward grabbing the prince by the sleeve of his arm and drag him with me into the mirror. He watches me in the reflection, his attention safely staying on my face. I turn and find Lincoln's attention traveling farther down my body.

"I'm taller." I face him.

My nose pretty well aligns with his and he leans forward till we're touching. "Would you look at that?"

"So you got taller?" Lincoln interjects. Kai stiffens and leans away. "Everything else is seriously identical."

"So my hair was always this perfect? My skin without flaws?"

"Yes."

I narrow my gaze and turn to Kai. He clasps his hands in front of him.

"I think your human eyes may have been broken." Kai tucks his hair behind his ear and leans forward, whispering out the corner of his sly smirk. "You've always been this lovely, Briar."

"I have wings!" I scream with a bewildered laugh.

"You're a true Shadow Fae. What did you expect?" Is the best Lincoln can offer.

My lips curl because I'm certain they are pulling my leg. I lean into the mirror, picking apart my appearance. My body, that I would typically consider not all that curvy unless I create some sort of optical illusion with clothing, is now more defined. I can't imagine that these men have both seen me like I am now.

"I don't believe either of you." My ears catch foreign footsteps, and I straighten as I narrow down where exactly the steps are coming from.

Someone is coming to fetch, Kai. Lincoln whispers only to me. His words in my head are quickly followed by a swift knock at the door.

"Duty calls." Kai bows low before me then escorts himself out of the room.

Lincoln places his hands on his lean hips and turns to the side to let him through, watching his brother as he walks away. There's a hush that falls in Kai's absence. The static between us is thick with unspoken words and thoughts we both ignore. The door clicks shut behind the prince and I can hear him and whoever came for him mumbling in the hallway.

I turn to Lincoln. His arms fill the sleeves of his button up shirt, making the curve of his biceps more apparent. It takes all of me not to reach for him.

"I'm glad you came."

Lincoln drops his arms, pinning me with a dark stare. I drop my chin. He sways as he walks, every movement predatory, every step full of staggering confidence. His gaze meets mine at my newfound height. My tongue darts out to moisten my bottom lip. Is it enough to convince him to kiss me? Or are we nothing now?

I don't want to be nothing. I want to be something,

anything, and everything with and to him. But he needs to fight for us. He needs to accept us. So the question then really becomes, does he want to be something?

The rough stubble on his cheek scratches against mine as he leans into me. "You and Kai seem to have really hit it off."

There isn't an ounce of me that's willing to pretend like we aren't attracted to each other or even that I don't want him. I've let life give me whatever I get and counted it as good enough. I'm new now. I'm wholly myself for the first time ever.

And I'm chasing what I want.

My arms slip over his wide shoulders, clasping firmly around his neck, pulling him toward my mouth. His hands don't hover in the polite way Kai's would. They grab ahold of my hips, helping me balance as I lean into him. Even through his clothing, he's warm against all my bare skin.

"Don't pretend like you aren't envious."

This time, for once, it isn't me who trembles. A shiver passes down Lincoln's spine and he straightens. His hands never leave my hips, though I fully expect him to step away from me. Lincoln is always putting distance between us when he thinks I'll make him vulnerable.

"I think you two are lovely together." His smile widens giving me the view of his perfectly white teeth. It's a feline smile. Smooth but deadly, like the careful steps of a killer. The only difference is that I'm no longer the victim. He is, he just doesn't know it yet.

I see you're still playing the same old games, Lincoln.

"We're... *friends.*" I clasp my hands over his, guiding them up over the curve of my body.

Don't tease me, Briar.

"In the same way you and I are friends?" His jaw is tight, his stare tensely set on my face.

"Do you think I'd let Kai touch me like this?"

His palms, much rougher than his brothers, catch on the fabric of the bra. Our hands graze over my breasts and then slip back down over my waist. Lincoln's Adam's apple bobs.

"I wouldn't expect you to wait around for me. Kai's a great match. It'd make my mother proud to see you two together."

"I have no intentions of marrying for power or to please some other court."

Lincoln tilts his body back, his chin lifting with an amused chuckle. It's all a game. Love is like chess to him. I wrap my fingers around his wrist, squeezing tightly in frustration.

"You're drunk on your new Fae abilities," there's a venomous hiss to his words as he rips his hands away. He rubs at his wrists, red from my grip.

Did I really squeeze so tight I left a mark? The red fades quickly, but the image is somehow burned into my mind's eye. I don't know my own strength.

"Or I know what I want."

I shove by him, letting our shoulders collide. My wings fan over him as I pass. I smile to myself, recognizing that hitting that steel frame body of his didn't make me feel as delicate and fragile as it normally does. His attention snags on the sheer blue skin of my wings.

Knowing I have a drawer full of mortal clothes, and needing a connection to my humanity I head for my dresser. *Before I'm drunk on my new Fae abilities.* I mock his words in my head, uncaring on if he hears or not.

No steps chase after me. No sulky or sarcastic remarks follow me into the next room. Lincoln's presence is still there inside my head, listening with intention

"Why did you come, Lincoln?" I shove my legs into a pair of dark jeans. When my legs poke out the bottom, I stare down at them.

Highwaters. I sure as hell got taller.

I growl, letting it rumble in my chest the way I'd heard Lincoln do before. It vibrates deep in my ribcage and rattles in my bones. Lincoln fists his hands at the sound. I can't see the man, but I can feel the way he wants to throw all his restraint out the window and gather me up in a tender kiss before he flings me to the bed and rips my clothes off.

"I thought my intention was clear. I was worried."

"Because I'm your investment, to get out of living under Cordelia's rule?" I accuse.

Lincoln takes a large step out of the bathroom. He watches, scrubbing at his not-quite-beard as I unbutton my pants and shimmy out of them. Fae clothes it is. So I walk by him again, I'll make him chase me all around this damn guest suite today. I roll my eyes at the expanse of the closet.

There's an entire rainbow of clothes here and any other girl would be swooning at the possibilities. They're exhausting. I reach for red, loving the way it catches Lincoln's thoughts.

"No," he grumbles.

His steps make the floorboards creak. He doesn't move toward me, but away, into the living space.

"No?" I say with mock surprise.

"I was fucking worried," he whispers. My new Fae hearing catches it with ease.

"And why would you be worried?"

"I thought we already established that I care about you. Why are you making me say it? Why do we need to say it?"

He's so insufferable! Would his little Iron Fae heart stop beating entirely if an ounce of compassion snuck out of his cruel mouth?

"I just need to know the answer." I tug the outfit, a corseted number that matches the undergarments splendidly, showing them off through the sheer material. Thick red fabric falls like a waterfall from the hips leaving the front open, though my legs are still covered by pants. So it's more like a pantsuit, I suppose. Even if the Fae acted like they didn't know that that was not so long ago.

I pause not sure how my new wings are supposed to fit into the garment... or not fit? Will I need an entirely new wardrobe?

Lincoln's sigh carries into my mind. *Relax the muscle. Consciously think about relaxing your wings.*

Closing my eyes, I focus on releasing the tension in each of my muscles. I sway as I focus solely on my back and the wings sprouting from it. After a moment they curl against my skin, flattening over my shoulders and hugging my hips once again. I blink my eyes open and carefully pull the outfit all the way up.

Well that's handy. And will work well to hide my wings when I need to... which might be all the time until I can manage the whole Cordelia situation.

And in this pant suite, I do feel rather business-y. Or really, like I'm ready to take care of business. Will the fondest of my new abilities, the parts of me that make me feel like I can take on the world, eventually wear off? Or will I feel like this forever? I hope it lasts forever. Instead of for the moment.

"Why do you care about me? Why do you care what happens to me?" I hold the pieces to my body and stroll into the living space.

Lincoln is spread out in a single seat, his legs relaxed and parted, his arms hanging against the armrests. His rolled-up sleeves reveal his vascular forearms. He clutches the side of the chair, making the veins in his hands swell. My eyes fall to stare.

"Zip me up?" I bat my eyes.

He stands. Blowing out a long breath, he grabs the zipper, pulling it up. As it zooms smoothly up the fabric, over my wings, he whispers, "You'll be the death of me."

"Or I'll be your saving grace." I twist and snatch up the extra fabric of his shirt making him press against me again. There is a boldness in the way he doesn't hide the bulge that's stiffening inside his pants. It only makes me want him more.

The classic Lincoln smirk tilts one half of his smile. "I'm always up for a good debate."

"You're avoiding the question."

"So is this where I'm supposed to admit that I'm madly in love with you?" He teases his nose along the edge of mine.

Madly. He's always madly. Madly in love might be a nice change.

"The very least you could do is allude to it."

Lincoln wiggles his brows but doesn't respond. Gently, he pulls one finger at a time off of his shirt. Then drops himself back into the chair.

"I don't know, I seem to fancy this mystery between us." He fiddles with his collar and the wrinkles I've created in his shirt with a frown. "Will they or wont they be together...? That's the question."

"You fancy making me insane is what you do." I storm back into the closet snatching up a matching pair of heels. I mumble curses of how frustrating men are as I seat myself across from Lincoln and strap them on. Once I'm thoroughly uncomfortable, I cross my legs and stare back at him.

"You look a little tense." His eyes fall half-hooded

"Let me guess, you'd be willing to help me release

some more energy? As if it has anything to do with my powers and not the *growing* need inside your pants?"

"Actually, releasing the energy of your pent-up sexual needs and desires is directly related to how well you're able to handle the magic. Why do you think we Fae treat sex as we do? We are not stuffy and stiff humans. You are no longer human."

The stuffy and stiff human side of me is more stubborn than anything. "I think, I won't be letting you help me release that sort of energy until you openly admit your feelings."

And stop fucking with mine.

"What feelings, again?" He pinches his brows together, feigning confusion, before his tongue slides over his teeth and he grins again.

I purse my lips. "Two can play at this game."

"Eh, I don't know. I'm not sure I'm into playing as you do." Lincoln rises from his chair. "Well, I best be on my way."

"You're leaving?" I jump too quickly from my seat.

He looks me up and down, knowingly. "I've got responsibilities to return to in the Shadow Court. I've got to make sure it doesn't fall apart. I'm doing this for you." He tucks my hair behind my ear. "Wouldn't want you taking your Court back and finding it in utter disarray." His broad back faces me as he moves quietly across the room.

"As your future queen I have two questions."

He swivels on his toes, bowing without dropping our

eye contact. "Yes, my queen?" His words are a rasp of a sound.

Wow. Why did I just shiver so hard?

"How's Jase?"

"Oh," he says, "he's doing well. I've checked in with him a time or two and he's basically spent the entire time complaining that he misses you and asking me personal questions about my brothers. So... same old Jase, I guess."

I smile softly. *Same old Jase. God, I miss him.* "I'll see him soon through, right?"

"Yes. Now that you have your powers, I'd say it's about damn time we start making some real moves. You're not so fragile anymore." He adds the last part a bit more quietly than the rest. "You... ah, had a second question?"

"Well, this isn't so much a question as it is a request."

He hums, bouncing on his feet as he waits.

"Don't put up your wall anymore."

Lincoln freezes.

"I want... I want to be a part of your day and I want you to be a part of mine. Share your thoughts with me and quit blocking me out."

"... it's for your own good. And mine."

He's making me insane.

"No." I shake my head. "You don't get to decide what's good for me and what's not anymore. It's my job to create those boundaries for myself."

He nods, just once, almost robotically.

"Is that it?"

"Yes."

Lincoln pockets his hands, escorting himself out of the room without a second glance. The door closes behind him, the wall he's put up so often slams into place. I blink at the roughness of the feeling. It's like he's a fucking teenager and I've just told him to come out of his bedroom for once and he's pissed about it.

I laugh lightly to myself, but it quickly fades as I become aware of the muddle of feelings Lincoln had waiting on the other side of the wall. Desire and want, drowned out by dedication and tradition, are all buried under a deep past of hurt and sorrow. It slams against my chest stealing away every ounce of breath.

It hurts. Being in Lincoln's head might actually destroy me, if I let it.

SMALL TALK ABOUT BIG THINGS

THERE ISN'T anything left to do alone in my room but fret. I'm chewing on my nails, trying to sort through Lincoln's mind. His thoughts are there, but awfully silent as he notices my presence. He only grows slightly more distant as he reaches the Shadow Court and busies himself with work. A distraction.

I should do the same.

My heels click with a newfound determination and strength. Even I'm not blind to the confidence this power is bringing me. As I'm reflecting, I push through the dining hall doors that have been closed. It's not exactly meal time, but I sure as heck am starving.

I stop when I enter, shocked to find all three of Lincoln's siblings stretched out in different positions at the dining room table. They leave many seats between one another. In the middle of the table, there is a small tray of fruit, a snack that appears as if they've already picked at.

Kai and Violet both turn to look back at me. Rowan's eyes don't even crack open. There's a book, face down, with the pages fanning out to hold his spot on the table next to his feet. He's angled in his seat, with his arms tucked behind his head, gently snoring. Though it's clear that he isn't supposed to be napping right now.

Violet drops the small embroidery she was working on. Kai sets down his pen from the long scroll he's marking on in front of him.

"Briar!" Violet says, oddly cheerful.

"I'm surprised to find you all in here. Lincoln left and I was just hungry so I thought I would stop by and see if I could get a meal." I finally let go of the doors and let them swing shut behind me, then tug the slight cream-colored jacket I found up over my shoulders to hide my wings.

"Of course, you're probably starving!" Kai waves a servant toward the kitchen. They scuttle out without question.

"You look so different!" The princess squeals, jumping out of her seat.

I take a step away, my back hitting the doors. "You're in an oddly good mood..."

"She had a *friend* over last night." Rowan finally cracks an eye, letting it drift quickly back closed. "They were up all night long fucking so loud I didn't catch a minute's rest."

"Shut up, you oversized squirrel. Do you know how

many times I had to listen to your pets screech as if you were killing them? Those are not the sounds of women being *pleased*, Rowan. You hire very bad actresses."

Rowan snorts but doesn't respond. Kai's cheeks redden as he listens. "Must you two fight in front of our guest like that? You don't have to show her the worst sides of you. Though I'm certain Rowan has made it his mission to scare Briar away."

"You don't need to come to my aid. It's fine." I intertwine my hands in front of me.

"You're right. I vividly remember you handling yourself well enough on our trip." Kai bites into his lip looking from me to Rowan.

"I'm just happy," Violet grimaces, "to not be working on that damn embroidery anymore. This is the perfect excuse to take a break!"

"Why are you all working in here?"

Violet stands in front of my view of the other two, examining me. Though, Kai still speaks around her. "We're hiding. Together."

"Mom's in full force today and our tutors have some pressure from her, so they are being painfully annoying." Violet clarifies, lifting a strand of my hair and spreading it out on her fingertips. "It's so... metallic."

"Kai and Lincoln told me I didn't look any different."

Violet barks a laugh and shoots Kai a disapproving look over her shoulder. She flicks her long black hair behind her, crinkling her nose. "My brothers are idiots who pay no attention to anything. You'd think from the way they've stared at you since you arrived from the Mortal Realm that they would notice differences as vast as these." She looks me up and down, sneering, "Dumb twits."

"I'd say, 'play nice', but I'm too shocked to pretend as if I care."

"You're taller too!" Violet snaps her fingers. "Wow, I can sort of see the whole 'Mortal Queen of endless beauty' now. Sort of." She squints at me. "If I turn my head just right and allow my vision to go all fuzzy."

"I'll take that as a compliment, I guess."

"You're fucking blind, Violet." Rowan sighs. "I bet if she tried, Briar could pull more men than you on your best night."

"Doubtful, but she would give me a run for my money, I suppose, *now*."

It's a fight not to roll my eyes at her.

The Princess pinches the fabric of my small cardigan and lifts it up from my shoulder. "No!" she squeals, dropping the material and covering her mouth with both of her hands. "You have wings! I haven't seen wings on a Fae since Cordelia went on her lunatic spree. No wonder you paired such a lovely dress with a cloth like that."

Rowan leans forward as if he wants to stand and take a peek at my new body part too, but his interest quickly dies with one stern glance from his brother.

A servant, clad in a pressed black uniform, emerges from the kitchen holding a steaming plate saving me from having to retort. Violet dismisses me in a sweep of her hands, but her gaze follows me.

Balancing the plate of food, the servant offers me a chair. I sweep my long skirt under me, adjusting myself next to Kai, content to not be sitting directly across from Violet. Kai's pen still remains on his scroll and stays there until I pick up my fork. The movement somehow reminds him that he too should be holding something.

"On top of all the pressure mother's giving us, your presence has got her panties in a new sort of bunch. I had to listen to her all morning complaining about having a human in our castle. Well now, she'll be complaining about Shadow Fae later, I'm sure."

"I don't understand." I shuffle the vegetables around on my plate. "Aren't you all adults? Why do you have tutors and such? Isn't your schooling over?"

"No." The princess snorts.

"I wish." Rowan says under his breath.

Kai looks from his sister, to his brother, and slowly back to me. "Our main schooling is done, yes. But it's pretty traditional for us to have continued learning until we take our place on a throne one day."

"And if you don't ever get a throne?"

"Ug. I don't want to think about that." Rowan slaps his hands over his face, dragging his features down.

"Then the learning and improvement never stops," Prince Kai adds softly. "As annoying as it is... it's good for us."

"Such the traditionalist," Violet growls.

I look down to my plate, admiring the thick cut of steak glazed over with butter. The smells drift up to my face, making my stomach scream in hunger. I push my fork into the meat and slice a bite off popping it into my mouth after only a second of blowing on it. It scorches my tongue as imagined, but the feeling dies quickly.

I'm healing. I think with revelation.

Being a human had so many downfalls, huh? Lincoln's voice fills my mind.

I jump in my seat. I'm quick to scold myself, I'm the one who demanded he be present with me and to let me be present with him and yet here I am surprised that he's acknowledged a thought. Perhaps, I'm the idiot. I mentally face-palm.

"Let me guess, Lincoln." Violet coos, lifting her embroidery ring. She scowls at me, then offers a much wearier expression to her sewing. "Tell my brother," she pushes the needle through the fabric aggressively. "That he left and if he wanted to spend time with you he should have stayed. I'm not sure why he even bothers. He doesn't stand a chance with you."

Lincoln is painfully silent.

"I'd beg to differ."

The Princess snaps her head up, her eyes wide as she gives me her full attention. She looks at me for a moment, before resuming her work. "That'll change once you are presented with all your options of Fae who aren't mixed breeds. Lincoln's a bottom tier lover. –Sorry, Linc—. There is a world of men more suited for a queen, ones that their people can respect and that will give you alliance."

The metal of my fork bends in my hand. I grip it with such ferocity that my knuckles are white and the muscles up my forearm visibly tense.

"I think you forget yourself." I grind out. "You forget that I'm the rightful queen."

"Ooh, sassy, I like it." Violet bats her lashes at me.

Kai's pen freezes. Rowan quietly lowers his boots from the table and glances between us.

"Are you two going to fight right now?" Rowan says with a slow smile.

"That's ridiculous." Violet laughs. "We're much more civilized than that. Plus, Lincoln isn't worth fighting over."

"Again, you're wrong."

I force myself to set my fork down, more concerned that I'd stab the sharp points of it into her pretty pale neck and the blue vein that runs down it.

Calm down. Lincoln reminds me. *You're not yet used to the way your body processes emotion, now. Laugh it off.*

Laugh it off?

"Ha. Ha. Ha," I say rigidly. Trying to calm myself, I take a long slow breath but the bitter rage of Lincoln's mistreatment, the frustration of the mistreatment of all Fae with mixed lineage, still glows with a scarily hot flame inside of me. They're just like me. I'm just like them. Violet's cutting remarks, all of their remarks, are against everything that I am too. Not just Lincoln.

At that thought, I feel Lincoln thoughts stir. A dark violent rage fills his thoughts, it stalls whatever conversation he is having with another guard in the Shadow Court.

"The Shadow Fae are my people." I start. "So we won't be talking down to them in my presence any longer. Understand? In fact, I'd appreciate it if you didn't speak about them, the way that you do, at all."

"I'll take it into consideration." The Princess gives me a fake smile.

"Yes, she will." Kai repeats nodding his head. "How about a change of subject?"

I narrow my gaze at Violet, who only relishes in the fact that she's getting under my skin. She may have gotten under Lincoln's too, which is quite unusual for him. Kai reaches from his seat, placing his hand on mine. He strokes his thumb over my skin as he was when I woke up today.

"Briar," he says in a hushed tone directed at me.

It takes me a minute to quit wishing a sudden and painful death for anyone who speaks against my people before I finally turn to look at him. I stare back into his golden gaze.

"What."

"I understand your concern... and the respect that you wish for yourself and your court, but it may take some time for us all to learn how to leash out tongues." His smile tilts upside down as he looks to Violet. "Especially for my sister."

"I'm taking offense to that," she quips.

"You're meant to." Kai lets my hand go and folds his hands across his slim waist as he tilts his head back against his seat.

Rowan roars a laugh, slapping the table. My fork bounces against the metal.

"But we have more relevant things to talk about," Kai says over his brother, who still cackles at his end of the table. "We can set up a meeting, now, with your court. Gives you a chance to meet the higher-ups and the people who will be directly advising you."

"Judging you," Rowan interjects.

Kai closes his eyes, inhaling slowly. It could be that I'm not the only one bothered by his siblings today. When he opens his eyes again, directly meeting my stare, he asks, "What do you think?"

"I think it's time." I sit up a little straighter. "Though it would do me a little good to get familiar with what I can do and how to do it first. I don't want to go in totally unprepared."

"With your magic, you mean?"

"Yes."

"I'm afraid, none of us will be quite qualified for that job. We've never been foreign to our powers. Lincoln might be the better one for the job." Kai sits forward, setting his hands on top of his work.

"Lincoln's not around to help." I grit out.

"Can't you too speak into each other's minds? Do that." Violet juts out her chin.

"It's not the same."

I try my best to relax my jaw, nervous that if I don't, I'll start shattering my own teeth. Lincoln being in my head is not the same as teaching me. It's just not. I'd learn better in person too. But I also can't keep pushing this off.

Every second I wait, more Fae are terrorized or killed by Cordelia. Any human that wanders in with an unknown lineage is slaughtered. There has to be an end. I will be her end. I mean, maybe she'll step down and we won't have to escalate the issue any more.... but I doubt it.

I shouldn't need protecting from people who want me on the throne anyways. Plus, Kai will be there. Possibly Rowan... okay probably Rowan too.

"Set the meeting." I finally agree. "But one condition..."

"About time you start acting like the queen." Rowan picks at his teeth, smirking at me.

"What's the condition?"

Damn it, Kai is so good at ignoring his siblings, I note. That's something I could use improvement on. I'm sure I'll have to ignore stupid people all the live long day as queen. I just have to think about it like how I made myself distant when I was in a foster home that wasn't so good to me, or one that I was determined not to be good in.

"I want to see Jase first." Not want, I need to. I had to be certain that everything is as they tell me it is. I would not be at ease until I knew he was safe. He's all I have left and I'll protect him till the day I die. Which, seeing as I'm half Fae, probably will be for a *very* long time.

"I think we can manage that." Prince Kai flattens his hands and pats at the scroll.

"Good because that's nonnegotiable."

"Damn," Rowan continues to cheer me on. "You learn fast, human."

Not human. *I think.*

"And Lincoln can come," I tack on.

Were you planning on inviting me or just assuming that I'll be there?

I bite my lip. *Would you like me to send a formal invite? Would that please you?*

You know what, it totally would.

I'll write it up but, I expect you to be there if I go through all the trouble.

"Lincoln can come, I suppose. Though I don't think the court will find it necessary and it may get you off on a slightly different foot than what they expect," Kai answers, while Lincoln and I talk amongst ourselves.

"Is the court not made of Shadow Fae? Why would they be bothered by the head of the guard being in attendance."

"The Shadow Fae Court does have some titled Shadow Fae in it..." Violet speaks in a tone that says she's annoyed that it even needs to be explained.

Unfortunately, all my Fae strengths did not come with the complete comprehensive guide to my court.

That I'll need to learn on my own. Still, I let her continue.

"There are other Fae. Pure Fae, who have been brought up their entire lives for the sole purpose of assisting the mixed breeds in a world that is fully Fae. Their opinions are valued above the rest. And that's without mentioning that Lincoln was a gift to Cordelia. His loyalty should be unquestionably reserved for her."

"His loyalty is only to Cordelia?" I repeat.

"I said, 'should be' don't go twisting my words like that." Violet's face puckers.

"I'm glad to see that your good mood has been spoiled like my sleep." Rowan points his gaze at his sister, pulling a braid over his shoulder and fiddling with the end of it.

I'll come. And it will be fine. I know how to handle the damn stuffy fools at this point. Don't worry about me while you make your decision. Lincoln's mind is split between listening in to our conversation and sitting through a small meeting on his end.

Kai and the others give me time to answer and I can see that they're waiting for me to be done with the conversation inside my head so that I can respond to them. That has to be very annoying, and judging by the look on their faces, it very much is. But I'll get better over time, I remind myself.

I pick my fork back up and with little effort straighten it back out again. I'm gentler now with my touch as I pick at my food that's finally cooled down. Pointing my fork, speared with another piece of meat, at Kai.

"Set the meeting," I say firmly. Then I smile, brilliant and wide.

Because I know that things are going to change for the better.

For me. For Lincoln.

For all of the Shadow Fae.

WICKED BITCH

Days went by before Kai was able to get word safely to the court about our planned meeting. Each one of them passed with such brutal slowness I swore time was going backwards. I filled my days with headaches from straining my concentration in mild and mainly unsuccessful attempts at magic. After days of trying the most I could manage was the appearance of looking different for only short periods of time. But like a mirage they would fade and I'd still be sitting in my same clothes.

Somedays I practiced leaping off the edge of my bed hoping my wings would flutter and lift me up off the ground. It rarely worked and when it did it was only for half a second. Even with a running start I couldn't quite get the rhythm to keep me steady and afloat before coming crashing down on my knees. It was the least I could do on my own to pass the time. Finally, the day had arrived for the meeting, and with equal importance, my chance to see Jase.

I'd changed my outfit nearly a thousand times—I have a thousand different options—and settled for a white gown. It made me look more regal, in my own opinion, though much more skin is shown than would be appropriate for the human world.

This dress only has enough non-sheer fabric, on the upper half, to cover up my nipples. Other than that, it's simply white glitter over boning that holds the structure of the dress. The neckline dips down revealing my belly button before the skirt gathers purposefully to look as if I'm constantly holding it up for me to walk. Which consequently, makes it much easier for me to walk.

That's partially why I chose the garment. I wouldn't want to introduce myself to the people who will be, in Rowan's words, judging me for the rest of my life and then fall flat on my face. Though, I do find it harder now to be that clumsy. My body's more aware of my surroundings at all times, not to mention, the upgrade comes with better balance.

A gift box arrived this morning, the contents of which I now have draped over my shoulders and down my back. Snow colored fur, spotted in greys and creamy off-whites, was fashioned into a simple shawl that clasps with a single diamond studded button at my neck. My wings will be a surprise today.

Kai, Rowan, and I have been stuffed into a small, unmarked carriage. It's remarkably... plain. Much less than I even imagined for a carriage that would belong to someone with little money. Much like my dress, we can see the construction of the vehicle from the inside. It's only mildly worrying that I swear I can see a nail inching out of one of the boards. No one else seems to even notice.

So instead, I look down at my dress. A few leaves cling to the bottom of the skirt in the back where it touched the trail leading to the portal. I'd learned on my own well enough, in my waiting for this event, how to use my powers to change my appearance. My forehead still shines with the effort of the challenge. I mean, I was able to do it.

To anyone who saw me on the streets before I stepped into the waiting carriage, I looked just as plain as any other Shadow Fae. A long plain skirt, a billowing blouse, thin slippers for shoes, and a light hooded vest that I covered my hair with so I wouldn't have to think about changing that. The moment the door closed I let my magic go and the dress expanded in the seat.

Both Kai and Rowan's pauper appearances dissolve as well. My gown even creeps into Rowan's lap, where he sits next to me. He gently pushes it away from him.

"If it bothers you, you could go sit next to Kai." I lean down and peel a brown leaf off my dress.

"And miss my chance to sit next to you? No thanks." He holds out his hand. "If you're nervous, I could provide you some comfort."

I turn to look out the window at the beautiful city of Calhutta. "Not today." *Not ever, I should say.*

"We'll be there shortly," Kai assures, ever the gentleman. "We're actually meeting in a place of worship."

That drew my attention. "A church?"

"Yes. Though it's the faith of the old, old, old, testament. You're probably unfamiliar."

I nod as if I understand. My knee bounces against the carriage floor. I'm just waiting to get to this church to see Jase. And Lincoln. Oh, and can't forget, I have to start trying to gain some sort of traction and following so that I can kick the wicked bitch out of the Shadow Court and off my throne.

"Stop it," Rowan crosses his arms. "You're bouncing the whole dang carriage."

"If you keep shaking your leg like that, the poor boy will get motion sick." Kai pouts out his bottom lip.

I give him the smallest of smiles, and fight to still the restlessness of my leg. Settling on folding my hands tightly in my lap, I turn to look back out the window. Rising high above buildings white brick glitters in what's left of the sun behind the clouds. High peaks look carefully crafted and lovingly managed and not at all what I would call an *old* church.

"Is that it?" I point.

Kai leans forward to look out the window. He rests his hand on my knee just long enough to give the church a quick glance and then sits back in his seat. My eyes stay strained on the spot his hand had just brushed. It's unlike him to touch me without asking instead of letting his hand hover like a proper prince.

"That's it." His attention never fully meets mine. He chews on his lip, lost deep in his own thoughts.

It could be that he's just as nervous about this as I am. I think to myself. Even his heartbeat seems to be beating just a bit faster than normal. Well, the normal I've gotten used to in the past couple of days.

The remainder of the ride is quiet. I've practiced saying 'hello' in my head more times than I can count. At this point it doesn't even feel like it's a word anymore. I'm sure I'll stutter over it when I get in front of the small crowd. Or Jase can listen to my examples. He's never without an opinion.

My body wrenches forward with the sudden stop of the carriage. Rowan's thick skull smacks against the bare wood behind him. He hisses through his teeth and rubs the spot.

"I'll get the door. The church has been gracious enough to host us, but with our need to be inconspicuous I've asked that no help be in the building." Kai fiddles with the door handle. It creaks but doesn't move.

"Fuddy old thing," he curses. He jiggles it a bit harder and after a loud snap the door pops open. "Very good."

Kai offers me his hand. I gather the sparkling white material of my skirt in my hand, lightly stepping out of the carriage. My shoes tap against smooth concrete.... or is it marble? I look closer. Dark spirals of color have been infused into the stone walkway. What at first I thought was plain rock could very well be legitimate marble.

Outside of the carriage, I have a better view of the church. The marbling of the walkway weaves up the church's steps that lead to a set of French doors. Each panel of glass is intricately painted depicting different scenes of angels and demons at war. The building as a whole is comparable to a mansion, with a couple of towers on either side that reach up toward the sky.

Rowan gets out behind me, gently guiding me forward as I gawk up at the marvelous building. I loop my hand into Kai's arm, admiring the stained windows.

"It's so lovely."

"Yes," The prince looks over his shoulder. "A very pretty church."

His odd demeanor, the tension riddling his posture, and the tone of his voice pulls me from the trance. I study the veins popping out of his neck.

"Are you sure you're okay?"

"Yes. Yeah." He says sarcastically, "I just know that this needs to go well and I'm a little nervous. There aren't many people in the streets right now so there aren't many witnesses to our entrance. Though with as beautiful as you look in that white dress, they may mistake you for a bride."

"She looks like a goddess from my angle." Rowan adds from a few steps down.

"Lincoln and Jase should be waiting for us in the basement. The members of the court should be here soon." Kai pulls the French doors open. "You'll have a limited amount of time alone."

Alone. The word drifts into my consciousness for all of three seconds before I suck in a quick breath. The marbling has not only carried up the stairs but it fills the church's entrance hall. The floor. The walls. All of it is marble. Specs of glitter shine back at us from within the stone as the sunlight follows us in.

This must have cost a fortune to build.

Kai leads me to another, smaller door. Rowan's boots squeak with every step, they match the beat of my own pulse. The door opens to a small stairwell. It's dark with the exception of the light that comes from under the door at the bottom. There are voices on the other side, too.

"Do I look okay?" Jase's voice is shaky, and I can already picture him fidgeting. It brings a smile to my face.

Lincoln's gruff voice follows, with little amusement. "No one is coming here to meet you. I'm not sure why you're so worried about how you look."

"Isn't your brother going to be here?"

Lincoln chuckles. "He already is."

"What?" Jase's voice raises an octave and his feet shuffle like he is turning toward the door.

I reach for the doorknob. Kai's hand, clammy and cold, collides with mine.

"Allow me," he suggests.

I swallow the butterflies from my stomach that creep up my throat. I let the light of the room pour over me as we leave the last step behind. I don't care to take in the room, or the surroundings, or politely allow Kai to let my hand go. No. All I see is Jase and his large child-like grin as his gaze meets mine. His smile falls, his jaw dropping. I rip my hand away from Kai, and sprint to him.

My cousin quickly collects himself and sweeps me up in his arms. "Holy shit! Briar. Holy shit!" he repeats, "You look amazing. You look so different."

"Same old me." I let go, pulling away and trapping his face between my palms. Giving myself a moment, I look him over from head to toe. Somehow, someone had gotten him into a suit, a nice one at that. It would rival something Kai would wear. "How are you? Are you okay? Cordelia hasn't done anything to you, has she?"

"No, no. Lincoln and Lylix helped me find my own home in Calhutta," Jase gently pulls my hands from his face and cups them between us. "I'm fine. How are *you?* You look like a fucking queen."

"She is a *fucking queen.*" Lincoln mumbles into a cup, taking a long sip.

I shoot him a look that he eagerly ignores. His brothers walk around us to lean against the same countertop Lincoln has propped himself against.

Jase lifts my chin, tilting my head this way and that. His eyes widen, almost fearful. "You look like you. But you don't look like you. It's...crazy."

"I'm me, I promise. But look..." I undo the clasp of the fur shawl long enough to show off the tip of my wings. Jase's eyes manage to open even wider and I quickly clasp the shawl again. "Wings," I whisper, grabbing his arms and giving him a little shake.

"Holy fuck."

It's hard to not touch him. To hold him. It's been so long that a small part of me is afraid to let him go, that he'll disappear as soon as I do. I squeeze his arms.

"Gentle." He squirms out of my grasp.

"Sorry, I'm getting used to the new strength. I forgot to treat you like you're fragile."

"I'm not fragile."

"Well, you are a little bit." I shrug. "I know you're Shadow Fae but... you're still you."

Jase squints at me. "I think this change may have also gone to your head." He taps his finger against my nose. My lips curl in annoyance. "You're very pretty, Briar, but don't start letting your ego swell."

I laugh, swatting his hand away from me. "Let me step off my high horse." Gently, I straighten his suit. We let a brief silence fall between us, both of us content to let this building feeling of joy layer over us.

Rowan tosses braids over his shoulder, and pushes his way between me and my cousin. He offers two glasses, sloshing with clear, bubbling, liquid. "The court is here." He smiles. "Have a drink, you'll need it."

I wrap my fingers around the cup, fog forming around my fingers on the chilled glass. Lifting it up to my face, I take a small breath. My nose crinkles. "Alcohol?"

"Yes," Rowan leans forward with a goofy grin. "To lighten the mood."

"Why is there so much alcohol in a church?" I say, but still lift the glass to my lips and drink a hearty size gulp. Over my cup, Lincoln makes eye contact. He lifts a single brow.

This goes far beyond the average stock for a Sunday communion.

"Aren't most religious people alcoholics?" Kai lifts his glass in salute.

"No... not if they're doing the whole church thing right." Jase cocks his head. He looks into the carbonated fluid with a high examination, ultimately tilting the glass and chugging a few mouthfuls down.

The drink lives somewhere between a wine and a whiskey, burning down my throat and warming my stomach. I hold the cup tightly between my hands.

Kai perks up. "They're here."

"How exciting." Jase beams. "You're going to wow them."

"What should I do? I haven't even gotten to ask you how I should present myself. How should I say hello?"

"What?" Jase's shoulders shake with a chuckle. Rowan's laugh echoes his. "Briar, you look wonderful. You *are* wonderful. Just say 'hi' like you do when you speak to me. Don't freak out."

"I'm not. I'm not freaking out."

You look like you are. Quit sweating. Lincoln's voice echoes.

Pursing my lips, I set the glass down, and adjust my dress around my feet. Voices chime at the top of the staircase. Jase's slim hands grab my shoulders and turn me to face the door.

"Smile," he whispers in my ear.

But don't smile too much or you'll look creepy. Lincoln adds.

You're not helping. I want to spin around and give him a dark glare, but I pin myself to the spot.

"I'll get the door." Kai swings and sashays toward the door. He grips the door handle, gesturing dramatically to me as it comes open.

Couples teeter excitedly down the stairs. Fae begin swarming the room talking over one another excitedly. As their eyes land on me they run to surround me. It's only a moment before unwelcome hands are touching me, prodding me.

"Um, hello." I stutter.

A skinny woman, more limbs than anything, picks up strands of my hair. "It's like spun gold." She coos.

"She *is* endlessly beautiful." A short man, stacked with muscles gasps.

"She must be our true queen."

"She looks just like her mother."

The compliments and close examinations of me repeat as someone picks up one of my arms and spins me as if we are in a dance. While I turn, I catch Lincoln rolling his eyes.

"My name is Malacoy." One man offers his hand, his face looks painfully puckered.

"Briar." I give him my hand, narrowly dodging

another woman who ducks under our arms inching closer to my face. "Can I help you?" I ask. Malacoy pushes his jacket behind him and turns my hand to kiss my palm.

The woman, with icy blonde curls pinned tightly to her scalp, touches her nose to mine. I take a step back. A perfume of what I recognize as the scent of cocoa floats around her.

"I think you are magnificent." Her sentence catches on her lisp.

"Thank you." I step back.

Lincoln takes another drink and snorts.

"Now watch this." Kai ushers himself into the middle of the crowd. His hands sweep up and over my shoulders clasping the diamond button before he unhooks my shawl all together. My wings lift up and off my shoulders, pushing the crowd away from me.

I thought this moment would be spectacular. I thought that it would make me relatable. But their oohs and ahs mixed with their prying gazes only makes me feel like a caged animal at the zoo. My embarrassment travels all through my body, even my arms turn red.

"They're stunning."

"Wings."

"Wow," They say all together.

"Okay, that's enough of that." I hear Lincoln's voice as he cuts through the gathering, taking my covering out of Kai's hands along the way. *Relax.* He reminds as he lowers the fur over my wings and buckles it once more.

Kai taps a metal spoon against his glass drawing their

attention toward him. As their attention shifts away a small wave of relief passes over me.

"Guests, I'm so glad that you have finally arrived. Please help yourself to some refreshments and we can get to our meeting shortly. Our Mortal Queen will have plenty of time to answer your questions as we make a plan to get her to her crown."

The small crowd of people starts to shift as they move to the counter. The group pushes Lincoln toward me. He stumbles, mumbling under his breath at their apathy to his appearance here. One of the court members bumps against his back, jostling Lincoln so much that his drink sloshes over his bare chest and drips down to his auburn trousers.

I sigh and reach across the counter, which now looks an awful lot like a small bartop with all this liquor stacked on top of it, and grab a towel. Jase holds his fine suit and steps away from Lincoln. He moves smoothly and stops only when he reaches Kai's side.

"What is your problem?" I run the cloth down Lincoln's chest, letting my fingers skim over every dip in his abs as I drag the rag lower.

With judgmental looks and a few murmurs, the crowd slowly disperses and sets themselves up on a small sitting arrangement of white velvet couches and chairs. The seats are cast with colorful light from the two arching stained glass windows that touch the ceiling. Underfoot the floor is the same slab of glittering marble and the walls are stacked glowing white stone. I'd probably stop to marvel at the beauty of the room and this place if Lincoln's attitude wasn't catching my attention so.

"I'm not sure what you're talking about." He slams the glass on the counter.

"The mockery of their flattery? The eye rolling?"

"You must be seeing things, Briar." His smile is sour.

Don't you dare pretend like you aren't acting like a brat.

A brat? You're calling me... a brat? HA. Lincoln narrows his gaze on me.

Ignoring his scrutiny, I look around for another room to step into. Across the sitting area there's a plain white wooden door. I shift around Lincoln, finding Kai.

"If you'll just excuse us for a minute, we'll be right back." I hold a finger up and point toward the door.

Kai's brows pinch together as he follows my finger. "You're going to..."

"Be right back," I snap, clamping my fingers around Lincoln's thick wrist and dragging him away. He growls, letting his feet snag against the floor with every step.

I give the crowd, anyone who's watching me, a sweet smile and a slight bow, before I fling open the door shoving Lincoln inside the dark room, closing us in together. My back hits a shelf and I step forward only to bump directly into Lincoln.

My hands fumble against the wall next to us, feeling for any sort of switch for a light that I do not find.

"I can't find the damn light switch."

"Do you need light to tell me why you've closed me in such a small space." His face grazes against my hair. "All I can smell is you and it's making me drunk faster than the alcohol."

My cheeks burn and I'm thankful he can't see me, at least not well enough to recognize the blush. His hands trace over my hips and settle against the smallest part of my waist. I try to take a step away, or adjust myself so we aren't on top of each other, but I only hit against more wall, more shelving. Items stacked behind me topple loudly as I move.

Damn it. There is no fucking room in here. The walls feel even tighter as my thoughts admit how closed in I feel. Every movement bumps against Lincoln who stands just as hard as any other wall.

Why is he standing so close?

Why don't you take a step back?" I ask.

"I can't. Why don't you just get to the point so we can go back out there and you can be praised by your biggest fans?"

"That's not what this is." I wag my finger against his chest.

Lincoln snatches my hand up in his warm palm. "That's what it looks like to me."

"Are you jealous of the attention everyone is giving me? What is it Lincoln? Be honest, I'd rather you say it then I go trolling through your mind to find out."

"What? No. I don't know, they keep saying you're a power of beauty but... you're the same to me."

Power of beauty? When did they even say that? I try to think back over the bombardment of greeting. I could hardly sort out who was who and what hand was touching me for a minute there. *Oh... and 'I'm the same' so... Okay. Insult.*

"No." He grips my hand tighter. "You're—You've always been a power of beauty. From the moment you tried to kick my ass the second we met. Power and beauty."

We're so close he only has to lean a hair forward for our lips to brush. His words repeat in my head, filling my chest with ballooning hope. I take a long slow inhale, soaking in his nearness. The hand that isn't tightly wrapped in his, brushes over his pecs. The light patch of hair is soft, curling around my fingers as I trail over his hard muscles. His heart races at the touch. The beating picked up by my new and improved senses.

"Do I make you nervous, Lincoln?" I whisper.

He laughs dryly. "No, of course not."

But the pounding of his soul slams harder against my fingertips.

"I can hear how your pulse jumps at my touch." In the dark, I feel my way up to touch at the scruffy stubble covering his jaw.

"You don't make me nervous." Lincoln hums, his mouth trailing to nip at my ear. I tilt my head allowing him access to my throat. His teeth scrape down my skin. "You make me insane."

His teeth bite down on my neck, not hard enough to

break the skin, but hard enough to feel like a claim. He kisses gently over the spot as I gasp and feel my knees going weak.

"I haven't stopped thinking about what it felt like to be with you." He breathes, letting his nose rub against mine. "Every second. Every hour. Every day. I want to bury myself in you."

Holding the back of his head, I weave my hands into his shaggy hair and pull him against me. I press my lips against him, letting my frustration and anger out in a passionate push and pull that he returns. He bites against my lip, before breaking away.

"Is it just the sex you think of then?" I pant. Because if it is, I'll have to draw the line here and now.

Please be more than the sex. Please. My mind begs of him. I open my mind, even if one part of me doesn't care if he lies to me, I know it's for my own good and to feel the truth behind whatever he says next.

"It was never just the sex." His words are a dark rasp he presses against my lips. He says it slowly, letting me poke and prod in his mind as he does. My spirit curls against his as the pleasure of his honesty vibrates between us.

Lincoln moans and tilts his head back as our minds caress. He tilts his hips, grinding his length against me. "Briar, I will ruin you." Everything in his voice, everything inside of his mind, crumbles with the walls that he's built between us.

He cares about my reputation. He cares about getting

the chance to rule the Shadow Court. But the selfish part of him that he tries to hide away, the part of him that wants to love me, to keep me all to himself, swells with every fingerless stroke against his mind.

"We'll make it work."

Lincoln's head snaps forward. Both arms snake around me, holding me close to him. He parts my lips with the swipe of his tongue, teasing and taunting me with a kiss. My lips are swollen with the rough bruise of his kisses that nip at me without a foreseeable end.

"It's selfish of me," he breathes.

"It's selfless of you."

I want you. My thoughts echo.

His cock throbs as I feel my thoughts register in his. A rough growl fills his chest, rising low somewhere deep inside of him. With both arms, he pulls the skirt of my dress up.

Yes. Please. Please. Please.

I cheer him on as the wetness between my legs soaks my thin lace underwear. His thumb hooks the band of my thong and tugs it down. Lincoln grabs a handful of my hair, tugging gently as he guides my mouth back to his.

"If I put my claim on you," He kisses me quickly before he cocks my head, kissing and biting along my jaw. "There will be push back from the court. There will be push back from my mother."

"Your mother is a bitch."

He smiles against me. "Let's not talk about her right now, though." His hand slips between my legs. "I'm going to claim you. I'm going to fuck you how you deserve to be fucked." His fingers part my sex, a small hum of approval emanating from him as he slips a couple of fingers deep inside of me. "I just hope you don't regret it because there is no turning back."

Lincoln's grip on my hair is all that really holds me up. Two fingers dip inside of me while his thumb circles my clit. Every single part of me becomes tight and on the edge of something too far off to reach. My brain is too foggy to think. Every fiber of me is too drawn to him to care about any repercussions. I just want him to do this, to do more, to touch me and to love me. To care for me.

To claim me.

A chorus of laughter comes from the other room. My gasp of a breath silences in an instant. It makes me aware of how close the Fae who are waiting to judge me are.

"Can't they hear us?" I rasp.

Lincoln pulls his hand out of me, leaving me raw and exposed. "Mmm, possibly," he whispers with a hint of amusement.

A wild, untamed, grin lifts my cheeks. I run my hands down his chest, unbuckling his pants, pushing them away, gripping his length between us. His breath hitches. I stroke again and again and again.

With my dress gathered around my hips, it makes it easier to lower myself to the ground. My feet knock against items that clinch together behind me as I rest on my knees. There's so much of him, I spit into both hands and stack them at the base of his cock. I lick my lips and bring my mouth over him. His shoulders hit the wall behind him, scattering whatever was behind him with a similar clatter.

Moving my hands in opposite directions, I run my tongue over his thick shaft, sucking, and plunging him in and out of my mouth. His fingers intertwine in my hair, gently at first... Rougher within seconds. There's a bead of precum on the edge that stains the taste of him with salt.

Wetness drips from my lips, coating every inch of his member, and making my hand slick against him. Lincoln yanks himself from me, pulling me up to standing.

"No," he cuts out. "This is not a moment for you to be bowing to me. You are the queen and should not be on your knees."

"I want to."

"Not as much as I want to."

Lincoln gives me a quick kiss, uncaring of the dampness around my mouth. He sinks below me, letting my skirt tent over him. My hand reaches for the wall and something clatters to the floor before I find my balance.

Fae talk amongst themselves on the other side of the thin door. The thought of getting caught sends a thrilling tremble down my spine. I grasp the shelf behind me as he guides my legs a bit further apart and runs his tongue over my wetness.

The tip of his tongue slices through me and circles as he gently sucks my clit. I squirm, trying to hold in the sounds that want to escape me. Lincoln buries his face between my thighs, messily lapping up all of my wetness as he creates so much more.

He presses all the right buttons, hooking a finger into me to pet at what I quickly realize is my G spot. It's a new feeling, to have someone else find my pleasure so easily, one none of my past lovers had ever been able to find.

Everything builds inside me all at once. It's a rush of sensations racing toward something so, so close.

This time I can't keep my moan in. Not when he strokes and taps against it while his tongue rocks against me in the perfect rhythm. He lets all the bubbling ecstasy inside me build, his mind rejoicing as my hips rock on their own accord. My legs tremble. Still he caresses me and flicks his tongue until an earth shattering orgasm consumes me.

Nearly unbearable pleasure rocks through my core, making me arch my back, every muscle inside of me clenching against his fingers. I cry out, the Fae on the other side of the door still chatting loudly amongst themselves like the melody to my song.

Lincoln gathers my skirt back in his hands, taking both of my thighs and lifting me from the floor. My lashes are still fluttering when a hard thickness presses against my clit.

And then he adjusts me once more against him before he slides ever so slowly inside.

I gasp while he groans and takes his time easing into me and stretching me.

Once he's buried deep inside, I rock against him. He

lowers his face into my chest, kissing my breasts carelessly. After a short moment, I begin grinding against him, thrusting him deeper and deeper. Our movements get rougher.

Faster.

The shadow of my last orgasm makes everything more sensitive. And every movement threatens to send me spiraling.

Lincoln's chest is slick with sweat and my hair sticks to the sides of my face. We gasp for air, our chests heaving against each other. He slams into me so hard my head hits the wall but the force of it is exactly what brings me to my peak. I want to scream with the sheer intensity of the waves drilling all through every single part of me. I can feel what he feels, all barriers of his mind broken and gone. It all adds to my release.

Forcefully, Lincoln's mouth clamps over mine, catching and quieting the shriek that starts to explode out of me as he makes me cum once more.

This man knows what he is doing.

"Fuck." He growls. "You're addicting, Briar."

He slams himself into me, pounding against my sex. Air wheezes from him as he fills me entirely. I can feel how close he is to finishing and it taunts me with want.

Through my own haze of bliss, I grind every part of my slickness against him, fucking him as deep as he can go until his lips part with the most dragging breath that never seems to fully reach his lungs.

Lincoln holds me against him, thrusting, quickly and

powerfully, until his body convulses. The strength of his orgasm rattles my mind and makes my muscles clench around his dick as it vibrates through me as much as it does him. The moan that rushes from my lips is more of a scream.

He lifts himself up, only to push as deep as he can go. Then, slowly, he pulls himself from me.

I feel empty without him. Gently, he sets me down on unsteady legs, but I have to lean heavily to keep myself upright. Rough fingers find my chin and pull me in for one last kiss.

"You're mine now. And no other man can claim you." He reaches above him and light flickers on.

Mine... I recall very clearly how Fae don't date.

They fuck.

I'm suddenly aware that what he and I have is more than fucking. Much, much more.

I blink, but my eyes adjust to the light so quickly, I realize it isn't necessary but habit. Lincoln bends to pull up his pants.

The walls felt so close, the room so small, because... it is. Cleaning supplies and brooms are carefully lined up on shelves or hung on hooks. A... a fucking broom closet?

Oh my God. I wonder how many of them knew I was taking Lincoln into a closet and not just a different room.

Did they hear the clatter of cleaning supplies and the probably louder clatter of my climax?

There is no hiding the crimson that creeps up my neck and stains my cheeks and my ears now. Lincoln smirks as reaches for a few rags that are folded behind my head. His callouses catch on my dress as he moves the skirt and uses a cloth to absorb all of the mess.

"We're in a fucking broom closet," I swear.

"I can also see that."

I pull up my underwear and push down my wrinkled dress. Lincoln smooths my hair and presses a slow kiss to my forehead.

"Well..." I swallow. "we have to go back out there sometime."

"We should go back out there now."

"How do I look?"

"Like you just got fucked," Lincoln whispers with a smile.

"Stop, no. You're supposed to make me feel better." I cover my hot cheeks.

He pulls my hands down. "You look lovely. Would you like me to open the door for you?"

"If you would be so kind." My voice is strained. The heat of the moment is quickly dissolving as my chest and stomach ball up with the familiar nervousness. It's magnified by the knowledge that even if they act clueless everyone in the next room likely knows what we've just done.

I hit the light, hoping that if they didn't know this was a closet, they would continue to not know. It eases some of my worries. Lincoln opens the door. As I step in front of him and into the next room, he twirls a strand of hair on his finger as if to reform the curl.

Jase's attention is immediately on me. His eyes bore into my skin, his lips pressed tightly to hold back a smile. The white of his teeth pokes out and he digs them into the flesh of his bottom lip as I flash my eyes in warning.

So maybe this wasn't the best look for an up and coming queen...

"She's back!" Someone cheers.

"I think you mean, *she's come*," Jase says under his breath with that same asshole smile.

My eyes widen but he's the only one who comments on that.

"Oh, I can't get over her beauty." Someone else says.

"I'm so eager to make her my queen. Gah, I'd be devoted if only because of how gorgeous she is," Another praises.

The praise rains down on me. I'm not able to hold eye contact with any one of them for long. I bounce my attention from one face to another, giving each of them a polite smile until I finally land on Kai. Just as we look at each other, he doesn't hold back his sly smile.

Kai ushers himself from his seat, moving swiftly towards the bar. "Let me get you both a drink, I think you could use it."

Don't overthink it, Lincoln reminds me. *Remember, we as Fae celebrate our sexuality. Honestly, we're lucky they didn't listen in, and then we'd come out to an orgy.*

In a church? Oh, God. I just had sex in a church. Maybe I do need that drink.

"Relax." Kai strolls over to us, two glasses in hand, a

knowing smirk lighting up his face. "Take a seat. We were just talking about how Queen Cordelia is planning another cleansing."

Kai places his hand on the small of my back, wheeling me into an empty seat in front of the gathered court. Lincoln steps quickly behind us. I lower into the chair, my body stiff despite the soft cushion of the seat.

Lincoln snatches Kai's arm, holding his gaze. "No more touching."

Kai grunts a shallow laugh, pulling out of Lincoln's grasp. The prince gives Lincoln a mocking bow. "Drink up, brother. You're much too rigid."

Awkwardly, I laugh too. I hold the new cup and lift it up to Lincoln. He tips his cup toward mine, letting our glasses chime together before we bring them to our lips. His eyes never leaving his brother. He hovers behind my chair. Together we both down a large portion of our drinks.

Kai pulls a chair over to my other side and leans forward on his seat, eager to listen. I scout the room for Rowan. The brothers who are supposed to protect me, as King Dravid had said. Rowan has perched himself on the arm of a high back chair that one of the ladies of the court has curled into. She chats fondly with him while he shamelessly flirts back. Their whispers, though each one is more cringy than the next, are almost soothing. Not *all* the attention is on me.

And at least he isn't trying to make advances on me.

"I thought I ended the cleansings once and for all?" I try to start the conversation again.

"You standing up to her did quell it for a time. But after you fled the court, she's lost her mind all over again." The woman with far too long arms and legs says.

"She's spiraling into madness." The man at her side confirms.

"More madness than she already existed in." His plain brown suit is stuffed with muscle, stretching taunt against him as the short man leans forward. "The seer she found should be arriving today after her long journey."

"Could she not portal to her?" I whisper to Ziko.

"She's not fond of portals." He shrugs.

"We'll fix this all soon enough!" Kai reminds everyone. "Firstly, we'll have to go out into the court and make sure they are aware that she is here. Then we can build her following, grow her support, rally the army against the queen!" He cheers.

The court claps gleefully along with him. Their faces mirror their excitement.

Then their features blur. I close my eyes tightly then open them again hoping to blink away the fuzziness. Lincoln puts his weight into my chair, leaning heavily against it.

"I'm making plans to dispatch my nephew into the city." Someone says, a male voice, but it sounds underwater and I can't pinpoint the location.

I think my anxiety is getting to me. Something's wrong. The thought floats in the back of my mind.

My arms and legs go slack, my head dizzying, so I lean back into the chair. Lincoln's hand falls to my shoulder, his fingers fumbling against my skin until he finally is able to hold onto me.

I think... we've been drugged. Lincoln agrees. *That or this bubbly is just... good.* He sighs loudly, with a content smile.

"Are you okay?" I recognize Jase's voice but the last of his question is drowned out.

Wood splinters fly as the door explodes.

And a battle cry roars as the sound of an army barrels into the room.

229

CHAINS AND WHIPS DON'T ALWAYS EXCITE ME

BARE-CHESTED MEN from the Shadow Court guard, I quickly recognize in my foggy thoughts, fill the room. Meaty hands seize up the court members who hold up their hands in suggestion of innocence and surrender. Delicate feminine screams rattle my ear drums as the guards snatch up the rebelling court and hold them roughly in place.

"What is happening?" One of the men snap.

Rowan slaps away a guard's hand and moves to stand in front of me. Kai's chair flings to the floor as he stands up in a blur of movement. My fingernails dig into the arms of the chair. I uncross my legs, adrenaline and fear making my heartbeat drum inside me, nervous if I stand, I'll fall back into my seat.

The red glittering dress pokes through my hazy vision faster than the recognition of who's wearing the garment.

Sparkling stones cascade down the curves of a swaggering queen. Queen Cordelia's blue eyes narrowly span over the room. She locks her gaze on me.

"You look positively... Fae." Her eyes flash in anger. "Guards," she screeches, "seize that traitor."

"No." Lincoln and Rowan shout at the same time.

Lincoln shoots forward as guards' bustle into movement. Rowan shifts, but stills only as the draw of a sword tucks against his neck. Kai holds the hilt of his dagger at an angle at his brother's throat.

"Don't move, Little Princling," Kai whispers into his ear.

"What are you doing?" I choke on the words, trying to pull myself up. Cordelia laughs at my efforts.

"I'm sorry, Cupcake." Kai pouts out his lip. "I wanted this to work between us, you've really been a doll, a great guest," he adds with dry humor, "but I knew when you visited the Iron Court the first time that Lincoln was going to claim you. I thought that maybe if I was patient, I could gain your affection in ways other than this silly friendship. So I've made a deal to get out from under my parents thumb. A deal to be king to finally get the power that I deserve." His mouth falls into a sneer.

Rowan struggles against his brother. "I can't believe you right now. You're a traitor!"

"The only traitor here is Miss Briar Anders." Cordelia sways her hips dramatically as she parts the crowd to make her way to me.

"Kai," I whisper, practically begging. "don't do this." I reach for him, my hands shaking and clammy. Kai leans himself and his brother away from me, only disdain is left in his gaze.

"You sealed your own fate. My mother has made arrangements for the Iron Court and Shadow Court to join as one, for Cordelia and I to wed. If we took her crown, no such arrangement could be made. I could never have your heart and you even said you won't marry for power." Kai spits toward Lincoln.

Lincoln's knees give out before me. The metal of his cuffs bounces off one another as he hands fall into his lap. His shoulders curl inward as I finally teeter to standing.

Cordelia reaches out a slender arm, she pokes at my chin softly, making my body sway before falling back into the chair. Air whooshes out of the cushions around me.

"I have my seer and we will confirm just exactly what you are. Either you're my long-lost sister who needs to be quickly put to rest. Or you're an imposter who should lose their head for their lie. Either way," She crosses her arms, satisfied. "By tomorrow evening you'll be dead."

"You evil witch!" Jase screams. "You can't touch her. I won't let you touch her."

"Shut up!" she shrieks. Her hand slices through the air, her palm colliding with Jase's cheek. His head snaps to the side, his skin red in the shape of her handprint. "Bring him as leverage." The queen barks at the guards.

There are multiple images of her in my vision, all of

them swaying and fighting with one another to orient me enough to understand where she's at. The queen reaches down, tapping a finger on Lincoln's forehead.

"You'll be quick to join her." Cordelia squats to Lincoln's level. She leans forward sniffing the air around him. She huffs a breath. "The smell of her is on your lips. You'll be lucky if I let you wash yourself of her before you join her in the grave." She grabs a fistful of his hair, pulling his attention to her.

Just as his face lifts to meet her glower, he stands, shoving her roughly with his palms. He's sluggish, but he moves to peel off the metal cuffs covering the iron under his skin. Lincoln's nearly successful before a hoard of his own guards clamp their hands over his arms.

His bellowing, angry scream roars through the air. Even I shy away from the sound.

"Mortal Queen." Cordelia turns to me. In a single second she darts forward, blurring in my vision, and wraps her hand around my throat. "I've wanted to do this for so long and I never had enough proof to keep the public at bay. Thank you for releasing me of the trouble of making your traitorous activity up."

She squeezes. Air barely manages to trickle down my throat and my hands rise to push against her arm.

"Let her go." Jase's voice is full of panic, powerful but shaky all at once.

"I will kill you myself for this, Kai." Rowan says to his brother.

"Shut up, you buffoon. She doesn't love you either." Kai presses the knife at his brother's throat drawing a thin line of blood.

I stand myself up on my toes trying to fight to keep myself up right, trying to find a way to get another breath. Cordelia flings me to the side.

Pain twists in my ankles as I fight to catch myself, but the beads of my dress scratch against the ground as I fall in a disgraceful heap. I'm only there long enough for my arms to lift me back up. Then the world blurs as multiple pairs of arms grab at me and drag me forward. They don't care to let me get my feet under me.

I search, trying to find some sort of strength within me, some flame left of the powers I know so little about. My body is nothing but an empty shell. Whatever Kai had laced our drinks with has robbed both Lincoln and I of our strength.

Marble steps slap against my knees and shins, the only thing that can keep my focus. Cordelia's already storming ahead, she flings her hands in the air and wind whips violently around us. A dark black hole appears against the church wall and she points her guards through.

"Take them to the castle. To the courtyard. Lincoln will learn his lesson and I'll burn this church to the ground."

With her court still trapped inside, I realize. Cordelia is going to kill the members of her court.

And Rowan.

Hot tears form against my eyelids. I open my mouth to helplessly oppose the decision. But the guards run forward into the portal and my body becomes weightless.

My cries resound between the two worlds. It's filled with a defeated sorrow and cut short as my knees crash against the ground. The material of the gown tears from the power of the movement and I'm certain that without my Fae side finally being released the fall would have broken both of my legs.

"Tie her up there. She's too weak to be any more of a bother." One guard says to the other.

"No," I say, fighting to rip myself from his arms.

He laughs, pulling me along like a child.

"I am the Mortal Queen. I am your true queen. Let me go. Let. Me. Go." My words slur together drowned out by Lincoln's roar.

Looking over my shoulder, a crowd has gathered. What looks like staff from the mansion has filled the valley behind the garden. Grass stains my white dress green and the dirt below it adds a line of brown.

The guards stretch Lincoln's arms across two poles, tying him to them, on his knees. One of them points to the crowd and I can only make out the word's 'traitor' and 'punishment' over the roaring in my ears.

Jase wrestles against a guard on the edge of the crowd. They stuff a gag into his mouth, shoving him into the dirt, pinning him to the ground under a guard's boot. The staff look from one to the other with wide fearful eyes. I can feel their attention moving between Lincoln and me.

Rope digs into my skin as the guard ties me to a wooden stake in the ground. Everything was set up for this. This wasn't just a last-minute confession Kai had given in hopes to sway Cordelia into marriage. This had been his plan for long enough for Cordelia to set the stage. Was all of our friendship an illusion made of smoke and mirrors?

Dark curling smog follows the queen as she emerges from the portal. She dusts ash from her hands, closing her fist and the portal at the same time.

A worried sob teeters from my lips. What of Kai? What of Rowan? What of my court?

A whip cracks. It tears my focus to one spot in pinpoint clarity. Skin splits down Lincoln's back, red blood pouring out the cut. He stretches against his bindings, pulling away from the pain in his back. My back arches too. The agony of the strike so loud inside his head, I can nearly feel it burning on my skin.

No. No. No. I can't watch this.

No. No. No. She can't win.

"Lincoln Ziko. You are charged with conspiring to hide a possible contender to the crown. You have betrayed my trust and the trust of this kingdom." The queen growls.

The whip cracks again. Lincoln cries out, the ropes groaning.

I'm here. I'm here, Lincoln. I chant.

Don't watch. He urges.

But I can't tear my gaze away. I can't look away without feeling like I'm leaving him alone. He's taking this punishment for me. I'm the reason he's hurting now.

"Cordelia don't you do this to him!" I scream. "It's me you want to tear down. It's me you should be punishing."

Stop it. Lincoln's thoughts scream. *STOP IT.*

"QUEEN!" Cordelia bellows. "You will call me queen. And I have my plans for you." She points a long shaking finger at me. "Hit him again."

The guard raises the whip and slashes it back down. Lincoln's screams replay through the valley. The crowd gasps, many holding their breath or taking a step back. But they can't leave. No, Cordelia needs an audience and they have no choice but to stay.

"No," I yell again, looking to the crowd. "I am your queen. I am your queen." I repeat the sentiment as the tears fall in streams against my cheeks, making the skin taut. "Stop hurting him. He's mine. And I love him."

Lincoln's shoulders shake, as he hunches forward, pulling the rope as far forward as they'll go. His pain lives inside his mind, angry and shameful.

Cordelia's face glows with purple anger. "Oh, you *love* him."

Her heels dig into the soft dirt of the earth and she storms towards Lincoln. Blood drips down his back, his skin flushed a bright pink. As she walks to him, she starts picking up the fabric of her skirt. It slides high up her thighs and she keeps pulling at the material.

She reaches for Lincoln's hair, pulling his face up toward the sky. He's slick with sweat and his cheeks are damp with unasked for tears, his hair clinging to the sheen of his forehead.

"Lincoln is mine. I *own* him." Cordelia says, her tone is calm. "I'll wash him clean of you. I'll fuck him till he forgets you exist."

My heartbeat stops.

Cordelia flings one of her legs over his shoulder, Lincoln's mouth opens as he groans in pain, her heel hitting the fresh cuts. The queen slips a hand under her skirt, pulls her panties to the side and presses Lincoln's face into her, burying him in her pussy.

I turn away. But my mind is still aware.

Panic. Shame. Disgust. It's all relevant and comes to life inside of Lincoln. His mental walls slam up with such force I can no longer see the world through his eyes. He's alone in this place of disgrace.

"Turn her to me. I want her to see my cum on his face."

The guard that hovers with me grabs my cheeks and turns me toward the scene. I press my eyes as closed as they can be, but the sounds... they persist.

Lincoln chokes and gags, desperate to pull away. I can also hear the slickness of the queen. The wet slap as she grinds against his face. She breathes heavily, moaning under her breath with every rock of her hips.

The crowd behind her is silent.

Warm fingers fight to pry my eyes open, giving me

glimpses of the wicked gratification on Cordelia's face. My stomach turns.

A pleasure filled cry, soaked in the satisfaction that I'm here to bear witness, croons from her red lips. She pants, riding the wave of her performance shamelessly.

My jaw is set so tightly the muscles in my neck and face protest. I only willingly open my eyes as her foot slams back to the ground. She gives me a satisfied smile, tilting Lincoln's head back. His lips, his cheeks, and his chin all shine. As she drops his head, he sags to the ground, spitting.

Her smile lights up her face in the most terrifying of ways. She enjoys this. The cruel queen gets off on her unconsented dominance.

Bile rises in my throat.

I'll fucking end her.

She watches me. Her laugh an airy taunt. She holds her gown up off the ground and dips her hand between her legs. With glistening fingers she points at me and turns back to Lincoln. Her red nails dig into his cheek making crescent indents in his skin as she forces his mouth open and runs her fingers over his tongue.

Lincoln's eyes are shut so tightly his skin crinkles with the exaggeration. Somehow, he is unmoving under her touch. Somewhere in the back of my mind I register the guards hold on me.

But my limbs have gone numb.

And I'm thrashing against the hold.

"I'll kill you." I hiss the promise.

Cordelia nods to the guard, leaving her fingers fish hooked inside Lincoln's mouth. "I'd like to see you try."

Then the guard behind him raises his whip and strikes again.

And again.

And again.

RATED R

Blood has dried against the rope that sits at my feet. Gently, I run my finger over my wrist, peeling off the left-over flakes of scabs. The skin is already smooth and new. Fae healing has quickly closed the cuts on my arms from working the ropes off of myself. Now, the dead skin is easily coming off.

I'm healed. But a little part of me will always be broken.

My white dress is now an off-putting shade of grey with streaks of green from being yanked across the grass of the valley. Strips of fabric dangle from the tattered edges of my gown. My only small, very minuscule, piece of satisfaction is that Kai had paid for this dress and now it's ruined. I fiddle with the undone hemming, my back aching for rest. But there isn't anywhere I can lean. I hiss, just shifting my legs against the wrought iron cage. My back and wings are exposed the small jacket long since disposed of by the guards.

Lincoln groans, pushing himself up from where he's been laying on his chest. His eyes flutter, practically rolling inside of his head as he moves. His cuts, much deeper than mine, are almost closed now. But it would be hours before the scabs fell away from his perfect skin.

He wipes his hand over his mouth and stills. The images, the feeling, the helplessness of Cordelia forcing herself on him—and so publicly—fills his thoughts. In turn, filling my thoughts.

My fists clench the material of my dress tight inside of them. I hate to relive it, to truly see it through his eyes, now. I hate that he had to go through with it at all.

Finally, his iron sliced gaze lands on me. "Briar." His eyes drift away as he whispers quietly. "I'm sorry. I'm..."

"I'm fine. That—all of that mess wasn't your fault." The moment I say it the sadness in his gaze swings to me and then drifts down to my wounds. "I'm fine," I say once more. I try to push my skirt over my legs to hide the red wounds. Lincoln's attention only follows my hands.

"Your legs are covered in blisters."

"Turns out that releasing my Fae half only... made my allergy worse."

It could be worse, I try to remind myself. Though honestly, I'm not sure how. My legs are dotted with a heated red rash that rises up off my skin from sitting in this iron cage swinging above what is about to be a large party.

The beatings got the better of Lincoln. They'd carried his unconscious body all the way from the valley to here. Dirt sticks to his face, clinging to the evidence of Cordelia's abuse. I was awake for it all. It's hard to look at him, but he needs to know that nothing's changed between us. I won't give my demon spawn half-sister the pleasure.

Lincoln pulls himself to the edge of the cage. The bars press against his cheeks. Under us, servants scurry to and from setting up tables and chairs and rolling out a sparkling red carpet. Presumably for the queen to walk down to the massive throne that's been brought from the room on the second level. Crystals are strung onto banners that they tack to the walls.

"Well, this is going to be grand," Lincoln groans, sitting up. He tosses a look over his shoulder trying to get a glance at his back. "How is it?"

"You have a bit more healing left to do. At least you're alive."

"Oh, there is still time for that to change. And I'm quite certain it will." He offers me a pathetic smile.

I run my finger over a metal bar feeling heat tingle up my skin from its acid touch. There's enough room in here they could have put us both in one.

"Honestly, these cages remind me of that damn sex club." I think out loud, thankful for the slightest distraction.

"Sex club?"

"Yeah, remember it's where Rowan and Kai took me and Jase?"

Nothing like making small talk while we dangle above our waiting deaths. Just try not to think about it. Yeah, maybe that will make this all go away, just don't think about it. Briar, you idiot.

"The night you kissed Rowan?"

"Rowan kissed me," I correct him.

"You let him kiss you."

"I thought that didn't bother you. But by all means, now is the time to get it all off your chest." I gesture drastically below us.

"I didn't *like* it. But I understood it. I even understood how you and Kai could be so... so flirty."

"You think," I laugh, "You think Kai and I were flirting."

"Yeah, and look where that got you." His brows lift so high they're hidden by his shag of bangs.

"Look where that got me? Now tell me how... how was I supposed to know that your brother was going to betray me to the Queen of the Shadow Court in exchange for a loveless marriage? You're his blood and *you* didn't even know."

"We're not talking about that, right now." Lincoln's hand fists and he hits himself in the forehead, closing his eyes tightly. "I can't believe my brother. I'll wring his neck when I get out of here."

"*If* you get out of here."

"We're getting out of here," he says sternly.

"Alright, if you say so." I shrug. I run my sweaty palms over my skirt, no longer caring if I made myself a mess. After a moment of silence, I whisper, "Do you think Rowan made it out?"

"I--" His Adam's apple bobs in his throat. "I hope so."

Quiet voices carry up to our cages. I don't need to press myself against the bars and burn my face to know that Cordelia's crowd is arriving. Servants stand at the ready with trays holding arrangements of bubbling drinks and food. Their scent mixes with sweat, blood, and magic inside my cage.

There is a moment of awe as they look up at the spectacle of us above them. Not one of them are the court members I'd met earlier in the day. Which leads me to wonder if this is the rest of her court or if there are truly that many Fae here ready to worship at her undeserving feet.

The room fills with Fae in their finery. Bellion stands near the throne, running a long skinny hand down his jacket as he watches the crowd. I look from him to Lincoln.

"Bellion was behind all the killings. Why is he still walking around like a free man?"

"I was... working on that," Lincoln says with an edge to his voice.

"I'm sure he'll be pleased to see this th—"

Our cages jolt from their positions against the ceiling. Both my hands instinctively fall against the iron to catch me, searing my palms with its poison. Lincoln's eyes widen as he looks at me. Fear rallies in the back of his mind but I can feel him fighting to stifle it down. Perhaps I'm the same way. Scared of death but refusing to acknowledge it.

"It's going to be okay," he says with determination through gritting teeth.

"Is that supposed to calm me or you?" I cradle my burning hands against my chest, barely able to hiss out the words.

"Both." He nods, holding on to the bars.

He looks the part of a criminal.

It's oddly attractive. I think all too quickly, trying to dismiss the thought so disconnected from my reality. Lincoln gives me a small smirk.

Dirt is embedded under his nails and smudged against his cheeks. His hair is both messily tossed on top of his head and matted to it. He's shirtless and breathing hard, his yellow eyes glowing with a dare.

Faces grow nearer as we descend. Their features are so well masked with excitement it takes me a minute to see their worry. Cordelia might think she has their loyalty, but fearful people will never be loyal until they feel safe. Fae smile up at us, but it's in their worried glances to one another that I find the mixed emotions. The gentle graze of hands giving out comforting touches. Mother's calling to their children to keep them close. Yes, Cordelia's opened up this part to all ages no matter the gore.

Cordelia, my death is going to be rated R because I'm not going down without a fight.

The world is no longer the haze of the drugged drink given to me by Kai. I can see everyone's faces so clearly. I can move so smoothly once again. The only thing keeping me from feeling my best at the foot of my death is the bastardly iron surrounding me, burning me.

As the cages come to a halt again, dangling just a few feet off the ground now, my legs are jostled, peeling skin that's melting into a sticky mess against the metal. A groan, I'd rather not allow, leaves me.

"So this is your Mortal Queen?" Bellion saunters forward, announcing to the crowd. "She doesn't look so powerful to me." The gangly man reaches through the bars, trying to lift my chin. I shift out of the way and he laughs. His long fingers snatch up a bar in the absence of my skin and he pulls then pushes my cage, spinning me violently.

There's nothing for me to do but hold on and hold down the nausea building in my stomach and rising like acid up my throat. Faces, decorations, the flash of lights all come and go. They blur together.

"Bellion, you fucking bastard, don't you dare touch her!" Lincoln bares his teeth, spitting his words out like thunder.

"Oh, Lincoln," the queen's right-hand man purrs, "You'll be dead before long and you'll no longer be a worry I need to babysit. The least you could do is make your death quiet for us."

Still, Bellion, juts out an arm. My exposed back, my wings, slam against the bars and my body stings with the burning blight of fire. The room doesn't move any longer, but I can't will myself to open my eyes.

"I'm fine, Lincoln. He'll have to do more than take me on a child's ride to hurt me," I manage.

There's an angry haze inside Lincoln's head. Unbreakable and focused on his frustration. He keeps his attention on Bellion. With one violent kick of his boot, Lincoln forces his cage to swing forward and he wraps his hand up in Bellion's white shirt, dragging the Fae back with him as momentum carries the cage backwards.

"Mark my words, I'll tear you limb from limb when I'm free."

Bellion's nose brushes against Lincoln's. He gives him a dry laugh, and begins peeling his fingers from his clothes. Splotches of mud and blood cling to the white button up and he tries to wipe it clean from him.

"Ah, I see our *guests* are being treated well." Cordelia's shrill voice coos from the other side of the room.

I blink open my eyes. Fae step back, creating a walkway for the queen. She's changed from her glittering red gown and replaced it with a sparkling white dress not entirely different from mine. As the crowd moves with the swiftness of the sea calling its tide away from the shore, she locks eyes with me.

My expression doesn't change. I don't give her the satisfaction of acknowledging her. So she flickers her gaze to Lincoln. Cordelia's hand snakes down her body, traveling over the curve of her breasts, the flat valley of her stomach, and down to cup her own sex.

"I'd like to thank you for pleasing me so, Lincoln." She gives him a small wink. "At least we know that these half-breeds can still do one thing."

Cordelia holds her slender hands up, tilting back with a cackle. The crowd laughs with her. Some more willingly than others. Air wheezes from Lincoln's lungs and he freezes in his crouched position.

"Silence." The queen demands. Her heels tap against the shining tiled floor as she crosses her legs with an exaggerated sway of her hips. The dress gleams with the sparkling innocence of a freshly fallen and undisturbed snow.

This is no innocent queen.

The chandeliers cast their light down, creating a spot light between our prisons. She comes to a stop, gripping the bars. With every sway the crowd murmurs amongst themselves.

"I'm so happy you both could join us for this wonderful celebration." Her voice is poisoned with false sincerity.

All talking comes to a full stop. A hush falls over the crowd, their attention pulled to the arching entrance of the room. The thrum of power travels through the ground. It rises, sparking at the bottom of our cages, crackling like small bolts of lightning.

I inhale sharply. Empty eyes framed in tan skin and

dark silky hair. A familiar tan tunic is wrapped around her slender body, outlined in a similar stormy energy. Maybe the volcano top wasn't stormy because that's just how the atmosphere is, maybe it's stormy because Zeve is the storm.

Don't say a word. Don't acknowledge her. Lincoln begs inside my mind.

I won't. I would never. I'm as strong as I am now because of this woman, and I can't imagine what my human body would be like after the day I'm having.

"You've finally made it!" Cordelia says pleasantly, letting our cages go as a spark snaps at her fingertips. "It took you far too long." She deadpans.

"I was... busy." Zeve responds. She watches the crowd with little amusement. Her eyes searching for something, for *someone*, I quickly realize as she skims past Lincoln and I.

"Come now, enjoy a drink. Have a snack."

"I'd rather get this over with. As you know, I'm highly sought after and my work has little end." Zeve steps forward, still barefoot, to lift up the sheer scarf of a man who stands tensely to the side. She fiddles with the fabric for only a breath before she drops it and strolls forward toward us.

"Very well." Cordelia snaps her fingers. "Guards."

Men, previously under Lincoln's command, bustle forward pushing through anyone in their way. They jostle the cages with little concern for the blisters that bubble on my skin with every single tilting movement. Large hands reach in, tugging me out.

It's almost a relief as the cold air hits my burning skin before the scraps of my dress fall back over my legs. My ankles cock at an odd angle as I'm pulled forward with my heels dragging against the ground.

Lincoln restrains himself as the men tug him forward. He is assured in every graceful movement, strong in the chording muscles of his jaw, fierce with the stern stare of his eyes.

I catch myself much quicker than my old body would have and lift my chin in defiance. I give the crowd my attention and watch the idea of having a new queen play out in their thoughts.

"You know the deal," Cordelia starts. "It's very clear that the girl is now very much...*Shadow Fae*, but I need to know from whom she was born. The specifics. I want to end this once and for all."

"What about him?" Zeve focuses on Lincoln. "He obviously isn't this Mortal Queen you're so fearful of.

"I'm not scared of the Mortal Queen." Cordelia takes a step closer to Zeve, who only gives her an amused grin before she herself takes another step closer to the queen. "She's a nuisance that needs to be dealt with. And as for the half-breed, he's a traitor. I'll end his life after he gets to watch his bitch die."

I know Cordelia means for her words to be cutting, or heartfelt in any way, but all I can think about is the fact that *I'm Lincoln's bitch*. Like damn, we're finally an item and Cordelia's about to slit my throat. So, it isn't so much an insult as it is exciting.

I toss Lincoln a soft smile. From my view inside his head, I know that he knows how I'm looking at him but he remains focused on Zeve.

"Shall I begin?" Zeve sighs.

"Yes, but one more thing." The queen spins on her heel, flicking her skirt behind her. Her head held high, her shoulders relaxed, and a content smile on her face. This is the ending she's been waiting for. "To ensure that you play nice with the seer, I have my guards at the ready." She points back to her throne.

Stomping footfalls make the rhyme of a song, an arguing male voice the lyrics. The queen's yes-men bring Jase forward and force him to his knees on her dais. Surprisingly, he looks more annoyed than scared. Perhaps at this point, I've gotten him out of so many messes he still has some sort of confidence I can get him out of this one.

This isn't one of those times, Jase. I don't think I can pull this one off. Cordelia isn't some jerk picking on you because your mother was a drug addict, or my foster mother who caught you stealing. I can't talk us out of this one.

"Now, be a good little kitten and hold still for the seer." The edge of her nail digs into the skin of my chin as she pinches me with a small shake.

"No, I want the man first." Zeve crosses her arms.

"Lincoln? I don't need his mind looked into."

"Yes. *Lincoln,*" she says his name as if it's a foreign language, "first. Or neither of them at all."

"Fine."

Bare skinned guards muscle Lincoln forward. Golden eyes, sparked with the zealous flame of life, stare into my soul as he speaks. "I won't let anything happen to you."

"Oh, don't feed the girl false hope." Cordelia laughs, stepping up to her seat. Once she nuzzles herself into the throne, she crosses her legs and gives Jase a slight pat on his head, pushing his blonde hair into his eyes. Jase leans as far away from her as the hovering guards allow.

"I imagine a man of your talent should know what to expect." Zeve says to Lincoln.

He gives her a tight nod, closing his eyes. Her slender hands cup his temples and an electric current sparks between them. Lincoln gasps, his mouth falling wide, his chest stretching forward, and his eyes flying open as lighting snaps within them.

"Lincoln!" His name falls from my lips and I can feel the presence of Zeve inside his mind... and then inside mine. I try to snap my mental barriers up to push away her clawing grasp, but she nudges them aside as if they are as light as a balloon bouncing through the breeze.

Be still, Briar. The seer sings. *I have already seen your past and your future. You are meant for that throne.*

I squeeze my eyes tightly shut. *I may be meant for the throne but my time here is running out. Cordelia will have both our heads.*

I'm calling in my favor. Lincoln's voice says sternly. His physical body sparks with a loud crackle of energy. He groans, making Cordelia giggle like a child.

I was hoping you'd say that. Zeve's voice is smooth and enchanting. Maybe it's how she was created or maybe it's the magic she uses but every word she speaks lightens the anxiety inside of me.

What do you mean? I demand.

Kai wasn't the only one who Zeve owed a favor.

Now when I say run... you run. Zeve says, echoing the command as she pulls herself from Lincoln's mind. His skin buzzes, glowing eerily bright from the power that just ran through him.

Zeve sighs, rubbing her hands together. "Queen Cordelia," she begins, "I'm afraid I have a slight variation to your plans for the evening." The crowd begins to murmur, glancing from one another in question as if their friends might have an answer for Zeve's insubordination. "You, my dear, are not fit for your throne."

Cordelia bolts out of her seat. "What is the meaning of this? You better hold your tongue before I have it cut off!"

"Be quiet!" Zeve yells, her deep voice booming like thunder inside the large hall. She thrusts out a hand, a blue bubble of zapping angry electricity forming around Cordelia. "It is destined that the Mortal Queen rises up and rules. Only she can bring peace to this land. We can never have peace with a crazed ruler like you. Your paranoia is rooted so deep, Cordelia Nightwaters, you can't even see how far you've fallen... how much farther you still have yet to fall."

"You will not make a mockery out of me." Cordelia's magic slams against Zeve's. "Guards, seize this traitor." She hisses, pushing against it again and again. Zeve's magic holds steady.

"Don't you move." Another song filled feminine voice rises. From the entrance of the room, Lylix storms forward, her body flickering in sync with Zeve's sparks. Lylix casts both hands in front of her, forming similar white orbs around the guards. Around us.

"*Run!*" Zeve whispers.

LOST

THE BACK of my skull connects with the arch of a guard's nose. My other hand already reaching for the other guard's throat before I turn and bring my knee up into his balls. It connects with a satisfying slap and dare I say... a pop.

A distant pain throbs in the back of my head. I don't stop to give them any more of my attention or cradle the annoying ache. I fling myself forward, wincing as her magic washes over me. The white of Lylix's bubble parts around me slamming shut the moment I'm through. The guards stumble forward only to shriek as the power bites back at them, holding them in place.

"What about Jase?" I breathe. Lincoln reaches me, taking my hand and pulling me forward, even as my attention is focused behind me.

"I'll take care of Jase," Lylix calls.

"Someone stop them!" Cordelia's voice is hoarse.

But we don't need Lylix or Zeve to trap the crowd in whatever sort of forcefield they've managed to create. Because the entire gathering, backs away, allowing us an easy exit.

"Mortal Queen." Their whispers rise to a chant, then grow to a resounding demand.

I tug against Lincoln's hand, even as he pulls me forward and our feet pound against the tile. The echoes of the crowd follow us.

"We can't just leave them."

"Zeve has a plan." Lincoln cuts out quickly. "We need to hurry. Cordelia has more guards than this and I know they're on their way. They couldn't miss that commotion."

What I had once admired, this large beautiful mansion, is now just a streak passing me by. There isn't any time to take in the grand molding or the golden details. I don't bother to give the rising staircase, the one I'd met Lincoln on so many times before, another once over.

Every breath, every heartbeat, every step, it's all leading me away from where it all began. The Shadow Court may be destined to be mine, but first I have to get away.

Running as a Fae is hardly any effort at all. I may not be as fast as Lincoln, who shoves open doors and pushes a few servants from our path, but I'd still be nothing more than blur across any human's vision. My muscles feel only the slightest fatigue. Which could be attributed to the after effects of Kai's drugs... or rather Bellion's if I had to guess.

We move out to the Argenti Garden, the sun falling toward the horizon. Commands are called in the castle behind us. The concerning sounds hard to pick out around the now shouted 'Mortal Queen' from the Shadow Fae Court.

"Keep going. Hold my hand. Don't let go." Lincoln doesn't so much as ask me to do as he says, as he begs. His mind is a buzzing of worry, of determination to get me out.

We weave in and out of the plants, brushing by the long flowing limbs of the Reminints tree that tries to cling to our clothing. The valley is clear of Fae but the long posts set up for punishment are still here. Lincoln's dried blood against the blades of grass that we crush under our feet.

Guards crash out of the mansion behind us, swords caught in their hands. "Get them dead or alive!" The command is passed through the small regimen and carried to us on the wind that pushes against our backs as if to guide our steps.

"Where are we going?" I yell.

"I don't know. Away from here." Lincoln's voice wavers as he runs.

"I thought Zeve had a plan!"

"Yeah, a plan to get us out of dying but not a plan on where to hide us."

We reach the edge of the forest, and I bat away a

jutting limb. I can't hear the sound of leaves and twigs over the blood rushing inside my ears. Even though I'm certain I can't hear the guards behind us either, the phrase 'dead or alive' echoes in my thoughts.

Our bodies twist and turn at incredible speeds, my balance keeping my heels from actually snapping my ankles as I leap over bushes. Lincoln yanks me harshly to the left.

"There's a spell just up ahead!" He points ahead of us. "It looks like a portal."

I follow his directions. Two trees have old swirling text carved into their trunks, they glow a brilliant neon green and the air between them shimmers.

"Where does it go to?"

"I guess we'll find out."

He holds my hand a little tighter and surges forward. "Take a step." He insists.

It reminds of Kai and the way he guided me through the portal from the Iron Court to the bottom of the Ganush Mountain range. That was when he was my friend, guiding me to my powers. Now he is the traitor to my crown. The brother who betrayed his own blood.

Will Kai feel remorse after Rowan's death in the old burning church? Or does he even feel at all?

The green glow of the portal is even closer now. A relief as we hear the sound of the guards gaining ground. It's my untrained pace that's letting them so near. I should have fought harder to learn about my powers, to train myself before this disaster of a meeting came to be.

I shouldn't have listened to Kai.

"Hold tight."

I squeeze Lincoln's hand, hard enough I'm worried I'll hear the crunch of bones. He doesn't even wince as he takes the final leap into the portal and pulls me through.

Time no longer exists. In the step from this part of the world into the next I've both breathed a thousand breaths and lived a thousand lives with the single inhale it takes for me to take an exaggerated step down. My foot lands in clean white sand. My body tilts forward while my heels sink awkwardly. Neither myself nor Lincoln can catch ourselves from the force of our entrance.

Our hands finally slip away from each other's, gravity dragging us down. Small particles of dust cling to my cheeks. I cough to expel any that have managed to settle in my lungs as I breathed them in.

Heat and perfect white light from the sky above us illuminates the sand like a thousand diamonds. Water tickles at my toes. With one hand, I feel for Lincoln, finding his leg. He sits up slowly, looking out at the great blue ocean before us that crashes with foaming white waves and fills the air with its crisp salty scent.

"Where are we?" I whisper.

Lincoln twists, his face paling to a shade I would compare to Lylix's ghostly color. "Nowhere good." He says at the same time as a blade is pulled from its sheath.

I turn slowly, following the singing sharpened edge that's tucked under Lincoln's chin and up the extended arm of its owner. Buckles and leathers are fitted to a curvy but lean frame, curling dark hair falls over the woman's shoulders. Behind the swordsmen are several more women who shift without sound to surround us, all with their swords pointed for us.

"The better question... is *who* are you? And where have you come from?" Her voice is a deep baritone, gravelly, with a hint of an old accent I can't quite place.

We may be out of Cordelia's grip but we haven't out run death just yet.

I stare down at the blades aimed at my heart.

Death surrounds us.

THE END

Thank you for reading book two of our epic fae romance!
The final book, *The Lost Fae* is now available!
Get your copy now!
The Lost Fae

The Villainous Wonderland Series

Into the Madness

Within the Wonder

Under the Lies

Origins of the Six

Academy of Six

Control of Five

Destruction of Two

Wrath of One

The Hopeless Series

Hopeless Magic

Hopeless Kingdom

Hopeless Realm

Hopeless Sacrifice

The Secrets of Shifters

The Darkest Wolves

The Sweetest Lies

The Royal Harem Series

The Hundred Year Curse

The Curse of the Sea

The Legend of the Cursed Princess

The Severed Souls Series

Darkness Rising

Darkness Consuming

Darkness Colliding

The Huntress Series

An Assassin's Death

An Assassin's Deception

An Assassin's Destiny

The Monsters and Miseries Series

Hellish Fae

Sinless Demons

Dr. Hyde's Prison for the Rare

Escaping Hallow Hill Academy

Surviving Hallow Hill Academy

Stand Alone Contemporary Romance

Hate Me Like You Do

ALSO BY REBECCA GREY

Paranormal Romance Books

The Cursed Kingdoms Series

The Cruel FAe King

The Cursed Fae King

The Crowned Fae Queen

The Ruined by Fae Saga

Ruined

Madness

Heartsick

Reverse Harem Books

The Royal Harem Series

The Hundred Year Curse

The Curse of the Sea

The Legend of the Cursed Princess

Stand Alone Contemporary Romance

Hate Me Like You Do

ABOUT A.K. KOONCE

A.K. Koonce is a USA Today bestselling author. She's a mom by day and a fantasy and paranormal romance writer by night. She keeps her fantastical stories in her mind on an endless loop while she tries her best to focus on her actual life and not that of the spectacular, but demanding, fictional characters who always fill her thoughts.

If you want more A.K. Koonce updates, deleted scenes, and giveaways, join her Newsletter or Facebook Reader Group!

AK Koonce Newsletter

AK Koonce Reading Between Realms Facebook Group

ABOUT REBECCA GREY

Rebecca Grey leads a busy life. Somewhere between raising two kids and daydreaming about being a reality television star, she writes. As a reader she enjoys books filled with arrogant boys, who she would never waste her time on in real life, and large fantasy or paranormal novels. Much of her love for these things are reflected in her books.

Printed in Great Britain
by Amazon